Tioba

And Other '

Arthur Colton

Alpha Editions

This edition published in 2023

ISBN : 9789362093370

Design and Setting By
Alpha Editions
www.alphaedis.com
Email - info@alphaedis.com

Contents

TIOBA

FROM among the birches and pines, where we pitched our moving tent, you looked over the flat meadow-lands; and through these went a river, slow and almost noiseless, wandering in the valley as if there were no necessity of arriving anywhere at appointed times. "What is the necessity?" it said softly to any that would listen. And there was none; so that for many days the white tent stood among the trees, overlooking the haycocks in the meadows. It was enough business in hand to study the philosophy and the subtle rhetoric of Still River.

Opposite rose a strangely ruined mountain-side. There was a nobly-poised head and plenteous chest, the head three thousand feet nearer the stars— which was little enough from their point of view, no doubt, but to us it seemed a symbol of something higher than the stars, something beyond them forever waiting and watching.

From its feet upward half a mile the mountain was one raw wound. The shivered roots and tree-trunks stuck out helplessly from reddish soil, boulders were crushed and piled in angry heaps, veins of granite ripped open—the skin and flesh of the mountain torn off with a curse, and the bones made a mockery. The wall of the precipice rose far above this desolation, and, beyond, the hazy forests went up a mile or more clear to the sky-line. The peak stood over all, not with triumph or with shame, but with the clouds and stars.

It was a cloudy day, with rifts of sunlight. An acre of light crept down the mountain: so you have seen, on the river-boats at night, the search-light feeling, fingering along the shore.

In the evening an Arcadian, an elderly man and garrulous, came up to see what it might be that glimmered among his pulp-trees. He was a surprise, and not as Arcadian as at first one might presume, for he sold milk and eggs and blueberries at a price to make one suddenly rich. His name was Fargus, and he it was whose hay-cutter clicked like a locust all day in the meadow-lands. He came and made himself amiable beside us, and confided anything we might care to know which experience had left with him.

"That's Tioba," he said. "That's the name of that mountain." And he told us the story of one whom he called "Jim Hawks," and of the fall of Tioba.

She's a skinned mountain [he said]. She got wet inside and slid. Still River used to run ten rods further in, and there was a cemetery, too, and Jim Hawks's place; and the cemetery's there yet, six rods underground, but the creek shied off and went through my plough-land scandalous.

Now, Jim Hawks was a get-there kind, with a clawed face—by a wildcat, yes, sir. Tioba got there; and Jim he was a wicked one. I've been forty years in this valley, with the Petersons and the Storrses and the Merimys at Canada Center, all good, quiet folk. And nothing happened to us, for we did nothing to blame, till Jim came, and Tioba ups and drops on him.

Now look at it, this valley! There've been landslides over beyond in Helder's valley, but there's only one in mine. Looks as if the devil gone spit on it. It's Jim Hawks's trail.

He come one day with a buckboard and a yellow horse, and he says:

"Sell me that land from here up the mountain."

"Who be you?" says I.

"Jim Hawks," says he, and that's all he appeared to know about it. And he bought the land, and put up a house close to the mountain, so you could throw a cat down his chimney if you wanted to, or two cats if you had 'em.

He was a long, swing-shouldered man, with a light-colored mustache and a kind of flat gray eye that you couldn't see into. You look into a man's eye naturally to see what his intentions are. Well, Jim Hawks's eye appeared to have nothing to say on the subject. And as to that, I told my wife it was none of our business if he didn't bring into the valley anything but his name and a bit of money sufficient.

He got his face clawed by a wildcat by being reckless with it; and he ran a deer into Helder's back yard once and shot it, and licked Helder for claiming the deer. He was the recklessest chap! He swings his fist into Helder's face, and he says:

"Shoot, if you got a gun. If you hain't, get out!"

I told Jim that was no place to put a house, on account of Tioba dropping rocks off herself whenever it rained hard and the soil got mushy. I told him Tioba'd as soon drop a rock on his head as into his gridiron.

You can't see Canada Center from here. There's a post-office there, and three houses, the Petersons', the Storrses' and the Merimys'. Merimy's house got a peaked roof on it. I see Jeaney Merimy climb it after her kitten a-yowling on the ridge. She wasn't but six years old then, and she was gritty the day she was born. Her mother—she's old Peterson's daughter—she whooped, and I fetched Jeaney down with Peterson's ladder. Jeaney Merimy grew up, and she was a tidy little thing. The Storrs boys calculated to marry her, one of 'em, only they weren't enterprising; and Jeaney ups and goes over to Eastport one day with Jim Hawks—cuts out early in the morning, and asks nobody. Pretty goings on in this valley! Then they come back when they were ready, and Jim says:

"What you got to say about it, Merimy?"

Merimy hadn't nothing to say about it, nor his wife hadn't nothing to say, nor Peterson, nor the Storrs boys. Dog-gone it! Nobody hadn't nothing to say; that is, they didn't say it to Jim.

That was five years ago, the spring they put up the Redman Hotel at Helder's. People's come into these parts now thicker'n bugs. They have a band that plays music at the Redman Hotel. But in my time I've seen sights. The bears used to scoop my chickens. You could hear wildcats 'most any night crying in the brush. I see a black bear come down Jumping Brook over there, slapping his toes in the water and grunting like a pig. Me, I was ploughing for buckwheat.

Jeaney Merimy went over to Eastport with her hair in a braid, and came back with it put up like a crow's nest on top of her head. She was a nice-looking girl, Jeaney, and born gritty, and it didn't do her any good.

I says to Jim: "Now, you're always looking for fighting," says I. "Now, me, I'm for peaceable doings. If you're looking for fighting any time, you start in beyond me.

"You!" says Jim. "I'd as soon scrap with a haystack."

I do know how it would be, doing with a haystack that way, but you take it from Jim's point of view, and you see it wouldn't be what he'd care for; and you take it from my point of view, and you see I didn't poke into Jim's business. That's natural good sense. Only I'm free to say he was a wicked one, 'stilling whiskey on the back side of Tioba, and filling up the Storrs boys with it, and them gone to the devil off East where the railroads are. And laying Peterson to his front door, drunk. My, he didn't know any more'n his front door! "He's my grandfather," says Jim. "That's the humor of it"— meaning he was Jeaney's grandfather. And mixing the singularest drinks, and putting 'em into an old man named Fargus, as ought to known better. My wife she said so, and she knew. I do' know what Jeaney Merimy thought, but I had my point of view on that. Jim got drunk himself on and off, and went wilder'n a wildcat, and slid over the mountains the Lord knows where. Pretty goings on in this valley!

This is a good climate if you add it all up and take the average. But sometimes it won't rain till you're gray waiting for it, and sometimes it will snow so the only way to get home is to stay inside, and sometimes it will rain like the bottom fallen out of a tub. The way of it is that when you've lived with it forty years you know how to add up and take the average.

That summer Tioba kept her head out of sight from June to September mainly. She kept it done up in cotton, as you might say, and she leaked in her joints surprising. She's a queer mountain that way. Every now and then she busts out a spring and dribbles down into Still River from a new place.

In September they were all dark days and drizzly nights, and there was often the two sounds of the wind on Tioba that you hear on a bad night. One of 'em is a kind of steady grumble and hiss that's made with the pine-needles and maybe the tons of leaves shaking and falling. The other is the toot of the wind in the gullies on edges of rock. But if you stand in the open on a bad night and listen, you'd think Tioba was talking to you. Maybe she is.

It come along the middle of September, and it was a bad night, drizzly, and Tioba talking double. I went over to the Hawkses' place early to borrow lantern-oil, and I saw Jeaney Merimy sitting over the fire alone, and the wind singing in the chimney. "Jim hasn't come," she says, speaking quiet; and she gets me the lantern-oil. After, when I went away, she didn't seem to notice; and what with the wind in the chimney, and Jeaney sitting alone with her big black eyes staring, and Tioba talking double, and the rain drizzling, and the night falling, I felt queer enough to expect a ghost to be standing at my gate. And I came along the road, and there *was* one!

Yes, sir; she was a woman in a gray, wet cloak, standing at my gate, and a horse and buggy in the middle of the road.

"'Mighty!" says I, and drops my oil-can smack in the mud.

"Does Mr. Hawks live here?" she says, seeing me standing like a tomfool in the mud.

"No, ma'am," says I. "That's his place across the flat half a mile. He ain't at home, but his wife is."

The wind blew her cloak around her sharp, and I could see her face, though it was more or less dark. She was some big and tall, and her face was white and wet with the rain. After a while she says:

"He's married?"

"Yes, ma'am. You'd better not—'Mighty, ma'am!" says I, "where you going?"

She swung herself into the buggy quicker'n women are apt to do, and she whops the horse around and hits him a lick, and off he goes, splashing and galloping. Me, I was beat. But I got so far as to think if she wasn't a ghost, maybe Jim Hawks would as lief she would be, and if she didn't drive more careful she'd be liable to oblige him that way. Because it stands to reason a woman don't come looking for a man on a bad night, and cut away like that, unless she has something uncommon on her mind. I heard the buggy-wheels and the splash of the horse dying away; and then there was nothing in the night but the drip of the rain and Tioba talking double—*um-hiss, toot-toot.*

Then I went into the house, and didn't tell my wife about it, she disliking Jim on account of his singular drinks, which had a tidy taste, but affecting a man sudden and surprising. My wife she went off to bed, and I sat by the fire, feeling like there was more wrong in the world than common. And I kept thinking of Jeaney Merimy sitting by herself off there beyond the rain, with the wind singing in the chimney, and Tioba groaning and tooting over her. Then there was the extra woman looking for Jim; and it seemed to me if I was looking for Jim on a dark night, I'd want to let him know beforehand it was all peaceable, so there wouldn't be a mistake, Jim being a sudden man and not particular. I had the extra woman on my mind, so that after some while it seemed to me she had come back and was driving *splish-splash* around my house, though it was only the wind. I was that foolish I kept counting how many times she went round the house, and it was more than forty; and sometimes she came so close to the front door I thought she'd come through it—*bang!*

Then somebody rapped sudden at the door, and I jumped, and my chair went slap under the table, and I says, "Come in," though I'd rather it would have stayed out, and in walks Jim Hawks. "Mighty!" says I. "I thought you was a horse and buggy."

He picked up my chair and sat in it himself, rather cool, and began to dry off.

"Horse and buggy?" says he. "Looking for me?"

I just nodded, seeing he appeared to know all about it.

"Saw 'em in Eastport," says he. "I suppose she's over there"—meaning his place. "Gone down the road! You don't say! Now, I might have known she wouldn't do what you might call a rational thing. Never could bet on that woman. If there was one of two things she'd be likely to do, she wouldn't do either of 'em."

"Well," says I, "speaking generally, what might she want of you?"

Jim looks at me kind of absent minded, rubbing his hair the wrong way.

"Now, look at it, Fargus," he says. "It ain't reasonable. Now, she and me, we got married about five years ago. And she had a brother named Tom Cheever, and Tom and I didn't agree, and naturally he got hurt; not but that he got well again—that is, partly. And she appeared to have different ideas from me, and she appeared to think she'd had enough of me, and I took that to be reasonable. Now, here she wants me to come back and behave myself, cool as you please. And me inquiring why, she acts like the country was too small for us both. I don't see it that way myself." And he shook his head, stretching his hands out over the fire.

"I don't see either end of it," says I. "You're a bad one, Jim, a downright bad one."

"That's so. It's Jeaney you mean," he says, looking kind of interested. "It'll be hell for Jeaney, won't it?"

The wind and rain was whooping round the house so we could hardly hear each other. It was like a wild thing trying to get in, which didn't know how to do it, and wouldn't give up; and then you'd hear like something whimpering, and little fingers tapping at the window-glass.

My opinion of Jim Hawks was that I didn't seem to get on to him, and that's my opinion up to now; and it appeared to me then that Jim might be the proper explanation himself of anything the extra woman did which seemed unreasonable; but I didn't tell him that, because I didn't see rightly what it would mean if I said it.

Jim got up and stretched his legs. "Now, I tell you, Fargus," says he, "I'm going to put the thing to Jeaney, being a clipper little woman, not to say sharp. If it comes to the worst, I daresay Canada Center will give us a burying; or if she wants to slide over the mountains with me, there's no trouble about it; or if she'd rather go her own way, and me mine, that's reasonable; or if she says to do nothing but hold the fort, why, that's all right, too, only Canada Center would be likely to take a hand, and then there'd surely be trouble, on account of me getting mad. Now, I have to say to you, Fargus, that you've been as friendly as a man could be, as things are; and maybe you've seen the last of me, and maybe you wouldn't mind if you had."

"Speaking generally," says I, "you're about right, Jim."

With that he laughed, and went out, pulling the door to hard against the storm.

Next day the rain came streaming down, and my cellar was flooded, and the valley was full of the noise of the flood brooks. I kept looking toward the Hawkses' place, having a kind of notion something would blow up there. It appeared to me there was too much gunpowder in that family for the house to stay quiet. Besides, I saw Tioba had been dropping rocks in the night, and there were new boulders around. One had ploughed through Jim's yard, and the road was cut up frightful. The boulder in Jim's yard looked as if it might be eight feet high. I told my wife the Hawkses ought to get out of there, and she said she didn't care, she being down on Jim on account of his mixed drinks, which had a way of getting under a man, I'm free to say, and heaving him up.

About four o'clock in the afternoon it come off misty, and I started over to tell Jim he'd better get out; and sudden I stops and looks, for there was a crowd coming from Canada Center—the Storrses and the Petersons and the Merimys, and the extra woman in a buggy with Henry Hall, who was county sheriff then. "Well, 'Mighty!" says I.

They pulled up in front of Jim's place, and I took it they were going to walk in and settle things prompt. But you see, when I got there, it was Jim a-standing by his door with his rifle, and the sheriff and Canada Center was squeezing themselves through the gate and Jim shooting off sideways at the pickets on his fence. And the sheriff ups and yelled:

"Here, you Jim Hawks! That ain't any way to do."

Then Jim walks down the road with his rifle over his arm, and Jeaney Merimy comes to the door. She looked some mad and some crying, a little of both.

"Hall," says he, "you turn your horse and go back where you come from. Maybe I'll see you by and by. The rest of you go back to Canada Center, and if Jeaney wants anything of you she'll come and say so. You go, now!"

And they went. The extra woman drove off with the sheriff, hanging her head, and the sheriff saying, "You'll have to come to time, Jim Hawks, soon or late." Jeaney Merimy sat in the door with her head hung down, too; and the only one as ought to have been ashamed, he was walking around uppish, like he meant to call down Tioba for throwing rocks into his yard. Then Jeaney sees me, and she says:

"You're all down on Jim. There's no one but me to stand up for Jim."

She began to cry, while Jim cocked his head and looked at her curious. And she kept saying, "There's no one but me to stand up for Jim."

That was a queer way for her to look at it.

Now, that night set in, like the one before, with a drizzling rain. It was the longest wet weather I ever knew. I kept going to the window to look at the light over at the Hawkses' and wonder what would come of it, till it made my wife nervous, and she's apt to be sharp when she's nervous, so I quit. And the way Tioba talked double that night was terrible—*um-hiss, toot-toot*, hour after hour; and no sleep for me and my wife, being nervous.

I do' know what time it was, or what we heard. All I know is, my wife jumps up with a yell, and I jumps up too, and I know we were terrible afraid and stood listening maybe a minute. It seemed like there was almost dead silence in the night, only the um-m went on, but no hissing and no tooting, and if there was any sound of the rain or wind I don't recollect it. And then, "Um!" says Tioba, louder and louder and *louder!* till there was no top nor bottom to it, and the whole infernal world went to pieces, and pitched me and my wife flat on the floor.

The first I knew, there was dead silence again; or maybe my hearing was upset, for soon after I began to hear the rain buzzing away quietly. Then I got up and took a lantern, and my wife grabs me.

"You ain't going a step!" says she, and the upshot was we both went, two old folks that was badly scared and bound to find out why. We went along the road, looking about us cautious; and of a sudden, where the road ought to be, we ran into a bank of mud that went up out of seeing in the night. Then my wife sat down square in the road and began a-crying, and I knew Tioba had fallen down.

Now, there's Tioba, and that's how she looked next morning, only worse—more mushy and generally clawed up, with the rain still falling dismal, and running little gullies in the mud like a million snakes.

According to my guess, Jim and Jeaney and the cemetery were about ten rods in, or maybe not more than eight. Anyway, I says to Peterson, and he agreed with me, that there wasn't any use for a funeral. I says: "God A'mighty buried 'em to suit himself." It looked like he didn't think much of the way Canada Center did its burying, seeing the cemetery was took in and buried over again. Peterson and me thought the same on that point. And we put up the white stone, sort of on top of things, that maybe you've noticed, and lumped the folk in the cemetery together, and put their names on it, and a general epitaph; but not being strong on the dates, we left them out mostly. We put Jeaney Merimy with her family, but Canada Center was singularly united against letting Jim in.

"You puts his name on no stone with me or mine," says Merimy, and I'm not saying but what he was right. Yes, sir; Merimy had feelings, naturally. But it seemed to me when a man was a hundred and fifty feet underground, more or less, there ought to be some charity; and maybe I had a weakness for Jim, though my wife wouldn't hear of him, on account of his drinks, which were slippery things. Anyway, I takes a chisel and a mallet, and I picks out a boulder on the slide a decent ways from Canada Center's monument, and I cuts in it, "Jim Hawks"; and then I cuts in it an epitaph that I made myself, and it's there yet:

HERE LIES JIM HAWKS, KILLED BY ROCKS.
HE DIDN'T ACT THE WAY HE OUGHT.
THAT'S ALL I'll SAY OF JIM.
HERE HE LIES, WHAT'S LEFT OF HIM.=

And I thought that stated the facts, though the second line didn't rhyme really even. Speaking generally, Tioba appeared to have dropped on things about the right time, and that being so, why not let it pass, granting Merimy had a right to his feelings?

Now, neither Sheriff Hall nor the extra woman showed up in the valley any more, so it seemed likely they had heard of Tioba falling, and agreed Jim wouldn't be any good, if they could find him. It was two weeks more before I saw the sheriff, him driving through, going over to Helder's. I saw him get out of his buggy to see the monument, and I went up after, and led him over to show Jim's epitaph, which I took to be a good epitaph, except the second line.

Now, what do you think he did? Why, he busted out a-haw-hawing ridiculous, and it made me mad.

"Shut up!" says I. "What's ailing you?"

"Haw-haw!" says he. "Jim ain't there! He's gone down the road."

"I believe you're a blamed liar," says I; and the sheriff sobered up, being mad himself, and he told me this.

"Jim Hawks," says he, "came into East-port that night, meaning business. He routed me out near twelve o'clock, and the lady staying at my house she came into it, too, and there we had it in the kitchen at twelve o'clock, the lady uncommon hot, and Jim steaming wet in his clothes and rather cool. He says: 'I'm backing Jeaney now, and she tells me to come in and settle it to let us alone, and she says we'll hand over all we've got and leave. That appears to be her idea, and being hers, I'll put it as my own.' Now, the lady, if you'd believe it, she took on fearful, and wouldn't hear to reason unless he'd go with her, though what her idea was of a happy time with Jim Hawks, the way he was likely to act, I give it up. But she cried and talked foolish, till I see Jim was awful bored, but I didn't see there was much for me to do. Then Jim got up at last, and laughed very unpleasant, and he says: 'It's too much bother. I'll go with you, Annie, but I think you're a fool.' And they left next morning, going south by train."

That's what Sheriff Hall said to me then and there. Well, now, I'm an old man, and I don't know as I'm particular clever, but it looks to me as if God A'mighty and Tioba had made a mistake between 'em. Else how come they hit at Jim Hawks so close as that and missed him? And what was the use of burying Jeaney Merimy eight rods deep, who was a good girl all her life, and was for standing up for Jim, and him leaving her because the extra woman got him disgusted? Maybe she'd rather Tioba would light on her, that being the case—maybe she would have; but she never knew what the case was.

That epitaph is there yet, as you might say, waiting for him to come and get under it; but it don't seem to have the right point now, and it don't state the facts any more, except the second line, which is more facts than rhyme. And Tioba is the messiest-look-ing mountain in these parts. And now, I say, Jim Hawks was in this valley little more than a year, and he blazed his trail through the Merimy family, and the Storrs family, and the Peterson family, and there's Tioba Mountain, and that's his trail.

No, sir; I don't get on to it. I hear Tioba talking double some nights, sort of uneasy, and it seems to me she isn't on to it either, and has her doubts maybe she throwed herself away. And there's the cemetery six to ten rods underground, with a monument to forty-five people on top, and an epitaph to Jim Hawks that ain't so, except the second line, there being no corpse to fit it.

Canada Center thinks they'd fit Jim to it if he came round again; but they wouldn't: for he was a wicked one, but sudden to act, and he was reckless, and he kept his luck. For Tioba drawed off and hit at him, slap! and he dodged her.

A MAN FOR A' THAT

COMPANY A was cut up at Antietam, so that there was not enough of it left for useful purposes, and Deacon Andrew Terrell became a member of Company G, which nicknamed him "'is huliness." Company A came from Dutchess County. There was a little white church in the village of Brewster, and a little white house with a meagre porch where that good woman, Mrs. Terrell, had stood and shed several tears as the deacon walked away down the street, looking extraordinary in his regimentals. She dried her eyes, settled down to her sewing in that quiet south window, and hoped he would remember to keep his feet dry and not lose the cough drops. That part of Dutchess County was a bit of New England spilled over. New England has been spilling over these many years.

The deacon took the cough drops regularly; he kept his gray chin beard trimmed with a pair of domestic scissors, and drilling never persuaded him to move his large frame with other than the same self-conscious restraint; his sallow face had the same set lines. There is something in the Saxon's blood that will not let him alter with circumstances, and it is by virtue of it that he conquers in the end.

But no doorkeeper in the house of God—the deacon's service in the meeting-house at Brewster—who should come perforce to dwell in the tents of wickedness would pretend to like it. Besides, Company G had no tents. It came from the lower wards of the great city. Dinkey Cott, that thin-legged, stunted, imp-faced, hardened little Bowery sprout, put his left fist in the deacon's eye the first day of their acquaintance, and swore in the pleasantest manner possible.

The deacon cuffed him, because he had been a schoolmaster in his day, and did not understand how he would be despised for knocking Dinkey down in that amateur fashion, and the lieutenant gave them both guard duty for fighting in the ranks.

The deacon declared "that young man Cott hadn't no moral ideas," and did his guard duty in bitterness and strict conscience to the last minute of it. Dinkey put his thumb to his nose and offered to show the lieutenant how the thing should have been done, and that big man laughed, and both forgot about the guard duty.

Dinkey had no sense whatever of personal dignity, which was partly what the deacon meant by "moral ideas," nor reverence for anything above or beneath. He did not harbor any special anger, either, and only enough malice to point his finger at the elder man, whenever he saw him, and snicker loudly to the entertainment of Company G.

Dinkey's early recollections had to do with the cobblestones of Mulberry Bend and bootblacking on Pearl Street. Deacon Terrell's began with a lonely farm where there were too many potato hills to hoe, a little schoolhouse where arithmetic was taught with a ferrule, a white meeting-house where the wrath of God was preached with enthusiasm; both seemed far enough away from the weary tramp, tramp, the picket duty, and the camp at last one misty night in thick woods on the Stafford hills, looking over the Rappahannock to the town of Fredericksburg.

What happened there was not clear to Company G. There seemed to be a deal of noise and hurrying about, cannon smoke in the valley and cannon smoke on the terraces across the valley. Somebody was building pontoon bridges, therefore it seemed likely somebody wanted to get across. They were having hard luck with the bridges. That was probably the enemy on the ridge beyond.

There seemed to be no end to him, anyway; up and down the valley, mile beyond mile, the same line of wooded heights and drifting smoke.

And the regiment found itself crossing a shaky pontoon bridge on a Saturday morning in the mist and climbing the bank into a most battered and tired-looking little town, which was smoldering sulkily with burned buildings and thrilling with enormous noise. There they waited for something else to happen. The deacon felt a lump in his throat, stopping his breath.

"Git out o' me tracks!" snickered Dinkey Cott behind him. "I'll step on yer."

Dinkey had never seemed more impish, unholy and incongruous. They seemed to stand there a long time. The shells kept howling and whizzing around; they howled till they burst, and then they whizzed. And now and then some one would cry out and fall. It was bad for the nerves. The men were growling.

"Aw, cap, give us a chance!"

"It ain't my fault, boys. I got to wait for orders, same as you."

Dinkey poked the deacon's legs with the butt of his rifle.

"Say, it's rotten, ain't it? Say, cully, my ma don't like me full o' holes. How's yours?"

The other gripped his rifle tight and thought of nothing in particular.

Was it five hours that passed, or twenty, or one? Then they started, and the town was gone behind their hurrying feet. Over a stretch of broken level, rush and tramp and gasping for breath; fences and rocks ahead, clumps of trees and gorges; ground growing rougher and steeper, but that was nothing. If there was anything in the way you went at it and left it behind. You plunged up a hill, and didn't notice it. You dove into a gully, and it wasn't there. Time was a liar, obstacles were scared and ran away. But half-way up the last pitch ran a turnpike, with a stone wall in front that spit fire and came nearer and nearer. It seemed creeping down viciously to meet you. Up, up, till the powder of the guns almost burned the deacon's face, and the smoke was so thick he could only see the red flashes.

And then suddenly he was alone. At least there was no one in sight, for the smoke was very thick. Company G all dead, or fallen, or gone back. There was a clump of brambles to his left. He dropped to the ground, crept behind it and lay still. The roar went on, the smoke rolled down over him and sometimes a bullet would clip through the brambles, but after a time the small fire dropped off little by little, though the cannon still boomed on.

His legs were numb and his heart beating his sides like a drum. The smoke was blowing away down the slope. He lifted his head and peered through the brambles; there was the stone wall not five rods away, all lined along the top with grimy faces. A thousand rifles within as many yards, wanting nothing better than to dig a round hole in him. He dropped his head and closed his eyes.

His thoughts were so stunned that the slowly lessening cannonade seemed like a dream, and he hardly noticed when it had ceased, and he began to hear voices, cries of wounded men and other men talking. There was a clump of trees to the right, and two or three crows in the treetops cawing familiarly. An hour or two must have passed, for the sun was down and the river mist creeping up. He lay on his back, staring blankly at the pale sky and shivering a little with the chill.

A group of men came down and stood on the rocks above. They could probably see him, but a man on his back with his toes up was nothing particular there. They talked with a soft drawl. "Doggonedest clean-up I ever saw."

"They hadn't no business to come up heah, yuh know. They come some distance, now."

"Shuah! We ain't huntin' rabbits. What'd yuh suppose?"

Then they went on.

The mist came up white and cold and covered it all over. He could not see the wall any longer, though he could hear the voices. He turned on his face and crawled along below the brambles and rocks to where the clump of trees stood with a deep hollow below them. They were chestnut trees. Some one was sitting in the hollow with his back against the roots.

During the rush Dinkey Cott fairly enjoyed himself. The sporting blood in him sang in his ears, an old song that the leopard knows, it may be, waiting in the mottled shadow, that the rider knows on the race course, the hunter in the snow—the song of a craving that only excitement satisfies. The smoke blew in his face. He went down a hollow and up the other side. Then something hot and sudden came into the middle of him and he rolled back against the roots of a great tree.

"Hully gee! I'm plunked!" he grumbled disgustedly.

For the time he felt no pain, but his blood ceased to sing in his ears. Everything seemed to settle down around him, blank and dull and angry. He felt as if either the army of the North or the army of the South had not treated him rightly. If they had given him a minute more he might have clubbed something worth while. He sat up against a tree, wondered what his chance was to pull through, thought it poor, and thought he would sell it for a drink.

The firing dropped off little by little, and the mist was coming up. Dinkey began to see sights. His face and hands were hot, and things seemed to be riproaring inside him generally. The mist was full of flickering lights, which presently seemed to be street lamps down the Bowery. The front windows of Reilly's saloon were glaring, and opposite was Gottstein's jewelry store, where he had happened to hit one Halligan in the eye for saying that Babby Reilly was his girl and not Dinkey's; and he bought Babby a 90-cent gold ring of Gottstein, which proved Halligan to be a liar. The cop saw him hit Halligan, too, and said nothing, being his friend. And Halligan enlisted in Company G with the rest of the boys, and was keeled over in the dark one night on picket duty, somewhere up country. All the gang went into Company G. The captain was one of the boys, and so was Pete Murphy, the big lieutenant. He was a sort of ward sub-boss, was Pete.

"Reilly, he's soured on me, Pete. I dun-no wot's got the ol' man."

The lights seemed to grow thick, till everything was ablaze.

"Aw, come off! Dis ain't de Bowery," he muttered, and started and rubbed his eyes.

The mist was cold and white all around him, ghostly and still, except that there was a low, continual mutter of voices above, and now and then a soft moan rose up from somewhere. And it seemed natural enough that a ghost should come creeping out of the ghostly mist, even that it should creep near to him and peer into his face, a ghost with a gray chin beard and haggard eyes.

"I'm going down," it whispered. "Come on. Don't make any noise."

"Hully gee!" thought Dinkey. "It's the Pope!"

A number of things occurred to him in confusion. The deacon did not see he was hit. He said to himself:

"I ain't no call to spoil 'is luck, if he is country."

He blinked a moment, then nodded and whispered hoarsely: "Go on."

The deacon crept away into the mist. Dinkey leaned back feebly and closed his eyes.

"Wished I'd die quick. It's rotten luck. Wished I could see Pete."

The deacon crept down about two hundred yards, then stopped and waited for the young man Cott. The night was closing in fast A cry in the darkness made him shiver. He had never imagined anything could be so desolate and sad. He thought he had better see what was the matter with Dinkey. He never could make out afterward why it had seemed necessary to look after Dinkey. There were hundreds of better men on the slopes. Dinkey might have passed him. It did not seem very sensible business to go back after that worthless little limb of Satan. The deacon never thought the adventure a credit to his judgment.

But he went back, guiding himself by the darker gloom of the trees against the sky, and groped his way down the hollow, and heard Dinkey muttering and babbling things without sense. It made the deacon mad to have to do with irresponsible people, such as go to sleep under the enemy's rifles and talk aloud in dreams. He pulled him roughly by the boots, and he fell over, babbling and muttering. Then it came upon the deacon that it was not sleep, but fever. He guessed the young man was hit somewhere. They had better be going, anyway. The Johnnies must have out a picket line somewhere. He slipped his hands under Dinkey and got up. He tried to climb out quietly, but fell against the bank. Some one took a shot at the noise, spattering the dirt under his nose. He lifted Dinkey higher and went on. Dinkey's mutterings ceased. He made no sound at all for a while, and at last said huskily:

"Wot's up?"

"It's me."

"Hully gee! Wot yer doin'?"

His voice was weak and thin now. He felt as if he were being pulled in two in the middle.

"Say, ol' man, I won't jolly yer. Les' find Pete. There's a minie ball messed up in me stomick awful."

"'Tain't far, Dinkey," said the deacon, gently.

And he thought of Pete Murphy's red, fleshy face and black, oily mustache. It occurred to him that he had noticed most men in Company G, if they fell into trouble, wanted to find Pete. He thought he should want to himself, though he could not tell why. If he happened to be killed anywhere he thought he should like Pete Murphy to tell his wife about it.

Dinkey lay limp and heavy in his arms. The wet blackness seemed like something pressed against his face. He could not realize that he was walking, though in the night, down the same slope to a river called the Rappahannock and a town called Fredericksburg. It was strange business for him, Deacon Terrell of Brewster, to be in, stumbling down the battlefield in the pit darkness, with a godless little brat like Dinkey Cott in his arms.

And why godless, if the same darkness were around us all, and the same light, while we lived, would come to all in the morning? It was borne upon the deacon that no man was elected to the salvation of the sun or condemned to the night apart from other men.

The deacon never could recall the details of his night's journey, except that he fell down more than once, and ran against stone walls in the dark. It seemed to him that he had gone through an unknown, supernatural country. Dinkey lay so quiet that he thought he might be dead, but he could not make up his mind to leave him. He wished he could find Pete Murphy. Pete would tell him if Dinkey was dead.

He walked not one mile, but several, in the blind night Dinkey had long been a limp weight. The last thing he said was, "Les' find Pete," and that was long before.

At last the deacon saw a little glow in the darkness, and, coming near, found a dying campfire with a few flames only flickering, and beside it two men asleep. He might have heard the ripple of the Rappahannock, but, being so worn and dull in his mind, he laid Dinkey down by the fire and fell heavily to sleep himself before he knew it.

When he woke Pete Murphy stood near him with a corporal and a guard. They were looking for the pieces of Company G. "Dead, ain't he?" said Pete.

The deacon got up and brushed his clothes. The two men who were sleeping woke up also, and they all stood around looking at Dinkey in awkward silence.

"Who's his folks?"

"Him!" said the big lieutenant. "He ain't got any folks. Tell you what, ol' man, I see a regiment drummer somewhere a minute ago. He'll do a roll over Dinkey, for luck, sure!"

They put Dinkey's coat over his face and buried him on the bank of the Rappahannock, and the drummer beat a roll over him.

Then they sat down on the bank and waited for the next thing.

The troops were moving back now across the bridge hurriedly. Company G had to take its turn. The deacon felt in his pockets and found the cough drops and Mrs. Terrell's scissors. He took a cough drop and fell to trimming his beard.

THE GREEN GRASSHOPPER

ANY one would have called Bobby Bell a comfortable boy—that is, any one who did not mind bugs; and I am sure I do not see why any one should mind bugs, except the kind that taste badly in raspberries and some other kinds. It was among the things that are entertaining to see Bobby Bell bobbing around among the buttercups looking for grasshoppers. Grasshoppers are interesting when you consider that they have heads like door knobs or green cheeses and legs with crooks to them. "Bobbing" means to go like Bobby Bell—that is, to go up and down, to talk to one's self, and not to hear any one shout, unless it is some one whom not to hear is to get into difficulties.

Across the Salem Road from Mr. Atherton Bell's house there were many level meadows of a pleasant greenness, as far as Cum-ming's alder swamp; and these meadows were called the Bow Meadows. If you take the alder swamp and the Bow Meadows together, they were like this: the swamp was mysterious and unvisited, except by those who went to fish in the Muck Hole for turtles and eels. Frogs with solemn voices lived in the swamp. Herons flew over it slowly, and herons also are uncanny affairs. We believed that the people of the swamp knew things it was not good to know, like witchcraft and the insides of the earth. In the meadows, on the other hand, there were any number of cheerful and busy creatures, some along the level of the buttercups, but most of them about the roots of the grasses. The people in the swamp were wet, cold, sluggish, and not a great many of them. The people of the meadows were dry, warm, continually doing something, and in number not to be calculated by any rule in Wentworth's Arithmetic.

So you see how different were the two, and how it comes about that the meadows were nearly the best places in the world to be in, both because of the society there, and because of the swamp near at hand and interesting to think about. So, too, you see why it was that Bobby Bell could be found almost any summer day "bobbing" for grasshoppers in the Bow Meadows— "bobbing" meaning to go up and down like Bobby Bell, to talk to one's self and not to hear any one shout; and "grasshoppers" being interesting because of their heads resembling door knobs or green cheeses, because of the crooks in their legs, and because of their extraordinary habit of jumping.

There were in Hagar at this time four ladies who lived at a little distance from the Salem Road and Mr. Atherton Bell's house, on a road which goes over a hill and off to a district called Scrabble Up and Down, where huckleberries and sweet fern mostly grow. They were known as the Tuttle Four Women, being old Mrs. Tuttle and the three Miss Tuttles, of whom Miss Rachel was the eldest.

It is easy to understand why Miss Rachel and the children of the village of Hagar did not get along well together, when you consider how clean she was, how she walked so as never to fall over anything, nor took any interest in squat tag, nor resembled the children of the village of Hagar in any respect. And so you can understand how it was that, when she came down the hill that Saturday afternoon and saw Bobby Bell through the bars in the Bow Meadows, she did not understand his actions, and disapproved of them, whatever they were.

The facts were these: In the first place a green grasshopper, who was reckless or had not been brought up rightly, had gone down Bobby's back next the skin, where he had no business to be; and naturally Bobby stood on his head to induce him to come out. That seems plain enough, for, if you are a grasshopper and down a boy's back, and the boy stands on his head, you almost always come out to see what he is about; because it makes you curious, if not ill, to be down a boy's back and have him stand on his head. Any one can see that. And this is the reason I had to explain about Miss Rachel, in order to show you why she did not understand it, nor understand what followed after.

In the next place, Bobby knew that when you go where you have no business to, you are sometimes spanked, but usually you are talked to unpleasantly, and tied up to something by the leg, and said to be in disgrace. Usually you are tied to the sewing machine, and "disgrace" means the corner of the sewing-room between the machine and the sofa. It never occurred to him but that this was the right and natural order of things. Very likely it is. It seemed so to Bobby.

Now it is difficult to spank a grasshopper properly. And so there was nothing to do but to tie him up and talk to him unpleasantly. That seems quite simple and plain. But the trouble was that it was a long time since Miss Rachel had stood on her head, or been spanked, or tied up to anything. This was unfortunate, of course. And when she saw Bobby stand violently on his head and then tie a string to a grasshopper, she thought it was extraordinary business, and probably bad, and she came up to the bars in haste.

"Bobby!" she said, "you naughty boy, are you pulling off that grasshopper's leg?"

Bobby thought this absurd. "Gasshoppers," he said calmly, "ithn't any good 'ith their legth off."

This was plain enough, too, because grasshoppers are intended to jump, and cannot jump without their legs; consequently it would be quite absurd to pull them off. Miss Rachel thought one could not know this without trying it, and especially know it in such a calm, matter-of-fact way as Bobby seemed to do, without trying it a vast number of times; therefore she became very much excited. "You wicked, wicked boy!" she cried. "I shall tell your father!" Then she went off.

Bobby wondered awhile what his father would say when Miss Rachel told him that grasshoppers were no good with their legs off. When Bobby told him that kind of thing, he generally chuckled to himself and called Bobby "a queer little chicken." If his father called Miss Rachel "a queer little chicken," Bobby felt that it would seem strange. But he had to look after the discipline of the grasshopper, and it is no use trying to think of two things at once. He tied the grasshopper to a mullein stalk and talked to him unpleasantly, and the grasshopper behaved very badly all the time; so that Bobby was disgusted and went away to leave him for a time—went down to the western end of the meadows, which is a drowsy place. And there it came about that he fell asleep, because his legs were tired, because the bees hummed continually, and because the sun was warm and the grass deep around him.

Miss Rachel went into the village and saw Mr. Atherton Bell on the steps of the post-office. He was much astonished at being attacked in such a disorderly manner by such an orderly person as Miss Rachel; but he admitted, when it was put to him, that pulling off the legs of grasshoppers was interfering with the rights of grasshoppers. Then Miss Rachel went on her way, thinking that a good seed had been sown and the morality of the community distinctly advanced.

The parents of other boys stood on the post-office steps in great number, for it was near mail-time; and here you might have seen what varieties of human nature there are. For some were taken with the conviction that the attraction of the Bow Meadows to their children was all connected with the legs of grasshoppers; some suspected it only, and were uneasy; some refused to imagine such a thing, and were indignant. But they nearly all started for the Bow Meadows with a vague idea of doing something, Mr. Atherton Bell and Father Durfey leading. It was not a well-planned expedition, nor did any one know what was intended to be done. They halted at the bars, but no Bobby Bell was in sight, nor did the Bow Meadows seem to have anything to say about the matter. The grasshoppers in sight had all the legs that rightly belonged to them. Mr. Atherton Bell got up on the wall and shouted for Bobby. Father Durfey climbed over the bars.

It happened that there was no one in the Bow Meadows at this time, except Bobby, Moses Durfey, Chub Leroy, and one other. Bobby was asleep, on account of the bumblebees humming in the sunlight; and the other three were far up the farther side, on account of an expedition through the alder swamp, supposing it to be Africa. There was a desperate battle somewhere; but the expedition turned out badly in the end, and in this place is neither here nor there. They heard Mr. Atherton Bell shouting, but they did not care about it. It is more to the point that Father Durfey, walking around in the grass, did not see the grasshopper who was tied to the mullein stalk and as mad as he could be. For when tied up in disgrace, one is always exceedingly mad at this point; but repentance comes afterwards. The grasshopper never got that far, for Father Durfey stepped on him with a boot as big as—big enough for Father Durfey to be comfortable in—so that the grasshopper was quite dead. It was to him as if a precipice were to fall on you, when you were thinking of something else. Then they all went away.

Bobby Bell woke up with a start, and was filled with remorse, remembering his grasshopper. The sun had slipped behind the shoulder of Windless Mountain. There was a faint light across the Bow Meadows, that made them sweet to look on, but a little ghostly. Also it was dark in the roots of the grasses, and difficult to find a green grasshopper who was dead; at least it would have been if he had not been tied to a mullein stalk. Bobby found him at last sunk deep in the turf, with his poor legs limp and crookless, and his head, which had been like a green cheese or a door knob, no longer looking even like the head of a grasshopper.

Then Bobby Bell sat down and wept. Miss Rachel, who had turned the corner and was half way up to the house of the Tuttle Four Women, heard him, and turned back to the bars. She wondered if Mr. Atherton Bell had not been too harsh. The Bow Meadows looked dim and mournful in the twilight. Miss Rachel was feeling a trifle sad about herself, too, as she sometimes did; and the round-cheeked cherub weeping in the wide shadowy meadows seemed to her something like her own life in the great world—not very well understood.

"He wath geen!" wailed Bobby, looking up at her, but not allowing his grief to be interrupted. "He wath my geen bug!"

Miss Rachel melted still further, without knowing why.

"What was green?"

She pulled down a bar and crawled through. She hoped Mr. Atherton Bell was not looking from a window, for it was difficult to avoid making one's self amusing to Mr. Atherton Bell. But Bobby was certainly in some kind of trouble.

"He'th dead!" wailed Bobby again. "He'th thtepped on!"

Miss Rachel bent over him stiffly. It was hard for one so austerely ladylike as Miss Rachel to seem gracious and compassionate, but she did pretty well.

"Oh, it's a grasshopper!" Then more severely: "Why did you tie him up?"

Bobby's sobs subsided into hiccoughs.

"It'th a disgace. I put him in disgace, and I forgotted him. He went down my back."

"Did you step on him?"

"N-O-O-O!" The hiccoughs rose into sobs again. "He wath the geenest gasshopper!"

This was not strictly true; there were others just as green; but it was a generous tribute to the dead and a credit to Bobby Bell that he felt that way.

Now there was much in all this that Miss Rachel did not understand; but she understood enough to feel sharp twinges for the wrong that she had done Bobby Bell, and whatever else may be said of Miss Rachel, up to her light she was square. In fact, I should say that she had an acute-angled conscience. It was more than square; it was one of those consciences that you are always spearing yourself on. She felt very humble, and went with Bobby Bell to dig a grave for the green grasshopper under the lee of the wall. She dug it herself with her parasol, thinking how she must go up with Bobby Bell, what she must say to Mr. Atherton Bell, and how painful it would be, because Mr. Atherton Bell was so easily amused.

Bobby patted the grave with his chubby palm and cooed contentedly. Then they went up the hill in the twilight hand in hand.

THE ENEMIES

THE great fluted pillars in Ramoth church were taken away. They interfered with the view and rental of the pews behind them. Albion Dee was loud and persuasive for removing them, and Jay Dee secret, shy and resistant against it. That was their habit and method of hostility.

Then in due season Jay Dee rented the first seat in the pew in front of Albion's pew. This was thought to be an act of hostility, subtle, noiseless, far-reaching.

He was a tall man, Jay Dee, and wore a wide flapping coat, had flowing white hair, and walked with a creeping step; a bachelor, a miser, he had gathered a property slowly with persistent fingers; a furtive, meditating, venerable man, with a gentle piping voice. He lived on the hill in the old house of the Dees, built in the last century by one "John Griswold Dee, who married Sarah Ballister and begat two sons," who respectively begat Jay and Albion Dee; and Albion founded Ironville, three or four houses in the hollow at the west of Diggory Gorge, and a bolt and nail factory. He was a red-faced, burly man, with short legs and thick neck, who sought determined means to ends, stood squarely and stated opinions.

The beginnings of the feud lay backward in time, little underground resentments that trickled and collected. In Albion they foamed up and disappeared. He called himself modern and progressive, and the bolt and nail factory was thought to be near bankruptcy. He liked to look men in the eyes. If one could not see the minister, one could not tell if he meant what he said, or preached shoddy doctrine. As regards all view and rental behind him, Jay Dee was as bad as one of the old fluted pillars. Albion could not see the minister. He felt the act to be an act of hostility.

But he was progressive, and interested at the time in a question of the service, as respected the choir which sang from the rear gallery. It seemed to him more determined and effective to hymnal devotion that the congregation should rise and turn around during the singing, to the end that congregation and choir might each see that all things were done decently. He fixed on the idea and found it written as an interlinear to his gospels, an imperative codicil to the duty of man.

But the congregation was satiated with change. They had still to make peace between their eyes and the new slender pillars, to convince themselves by contemplation that the church was still not unstable, not doctrinally weaker.

So it came about that Albion Dee stood up sternly and faced the choir alone, with the old red, fearless, Protestant face one knows of Luther and Cromwell. The congregation thought him within his rights there to bear witness to his conviction. Sabbaths came and went in Ramoth peacefully, milestones of the passing time, and all seemed well.

Pseudo-classic architecture is a pale, inhuman allegory of forgotten meaning. If buildings like Ramoth church could in some plastic way assimilate their communicants, what gargoyles would be about the cornices, what wall paintings of patient saints, mystical and realistic. On one of the roof cornices of an old church in France is the carved stone face of a demon with horns and a forked tongue, and around its eyes a wrinkled smile of immense kindness. And within the church is the mural painting of a saint, some Beata Ursula or Catherine, with upturned eyes; a likeable girl, capable of her saintship, of turning up her eyes with sincerity because it fell to her to see a celestial vision; as capable of a blush and twittering laugh, and the better for her capabilities.

It is not stated what Albion symbolized. He stood overtopping the bonnets and the gray heads of deacons, respected by the pews, popular with the choir, protesting his conviction.

And all the while secretly, with haunch and elbow, he nudged, bumped and rubbed the shoulders and silvery head of Jay Dee. It is here claimed that he stood there in the conviction that it was his duty so to testify. It is not denied that he so bumped and squatted against Jay Dee, cautiously, but with relish and pleasure.

In the bowed silver head, behind the shy, persistent eyes of Jay Dee, what were his thoughts, his purposes, coiling and constricting? None but the two were aware of the locked throat grip of the spirit. In the droning Sabbath peace the congregation pursued the minister through the subdivisions of his text, and dragged the hymn behind the dragging choir.

It was a June day and the orioles gurgled their warm nesting notes in the maples. The boys in the gallery searched the surface of the quiet assembly for points of interest; only here and there nodding heads, wavering fans, glazed, abstracted eyes. They twisted and yawned. What to them were brethren in unity, or the exegesis of a text, as if one were to count and classify, prickle by prickle, to no purpose the irritating points of a chestnut burr? The sermon drowsed to its close. The choir and Albion rose. It was an outworn sight now, little more curious than Monday morning. The sunlight shone through the side windows, slanting down over the young, worldly and impatient, and one selected ray fell on Jay Dee's hair with spiritual radiance, and on Albion's red face, turned choirward for a testimony.

Suddenly Albion gave a guttural shout. He turned, he grasped Jay Dee's collar, dragged him headlong into the aisle, and shook him to and fro, protesting, "You stuck me! I'll teach you!"

His red face worked with passion; Jay Dee's venerable head bobbed, helpless, mild, piteous. The choir broke down. The minister rose with lifted hands and open mouth, the gallery in revelry, the body of the church in exclamatory confusion. Albion saw outstretched hands approaching, left his enemy, and hat in hand strode down the aisle with red, glowering face, testifying, "He stuck me."

Jay Dee sat on the floor, his meek head swaying dizzily.

On Monday morning Albion set out for Hamilton down the narrow valley of the Pilgrim River. The sudden hills hid him and his purposes from Ramoth. He came in time to sit in the office of Simeon Ballister, and Simeon's eyes gleamed. He took notes and snuffed the battle afar.

"Ha! Witnesses to pin protruding from coat in region adjoining haunch. Hum! Affidavits to actual puncture of inflamed character, arguing possibly venom of pin. Ha! Hum! Motive of concurrent animosity. A very respectable case. I will come up and see your witnesses—Ha!—in a day or two. Good morning."

Ballister was a shining light in the county courts in those days, but few speak of him now. Yet he wrote a Life of Byron, a History of Hamilton County, and talked a half century with unflagging charm. Those who remember will have in mind his long white beard and inflamed and swollen nose, his voice of varied melody. Alien whiskey and natural indolence kept his fame local. His voice is silent forever that once rose in the court-rooms like a fountain shot with rainbow fancies, in musical enchantment, in liquid cadence. "I have laid open, gentlemen, the secret of a human heart, shadowed and mourning, to the illumination of your justice. You are the repository and temple of that sacred light. Not merely as a plaintiff, a petitioner, my client comes; but as a worshipper, in reverence of your function, he approaches the balm and radiance of that steadfast torch and vestal fire of civilization, an intelligent jury." Such was Ballister's inspired manner, such his habit of rhythm and climax, whenever he found twenty-four eyes fixed on his swollen nose, the fiery mesmeric core of his oratory beaconing juries to follow it and discover truth.

But the Case of Dee v. Dee came only before a justice of the peace, in the Town Hall of Ramoth, and Justice Kernegan was but a stout man with hairy ears and round, spectacled, benevolent eyes. Jay Dee brought no advocate. His silvery hair floated about his head. His pale eyes gazed in mild terror at Ballister. He said it must have been a wasp stung Albion.

"A wasp, sir! Your Honor, does a wasp carry for penetration, for puncture, for malignant attack or justifiable defence, for any purpose whatsoever, a brass pin of palpable human manufacture, drawn, headed and pointed by machinery, such as was inserted in my client's person? Does the defendant wish your Honor to infer that wasps carry papers of brass pins in their anatomies? I will ask the defendant, whose venerable though dishonored head bears witness to his age, if, in his long experience, he has ever met a wasp of such military outfit and arsenal? Not a wasp, your Honor, but a serpent; a serpent in human form."

Jay Dee had no answer to all this. He murmured—

"Sat on me."

"I didn't catch your remark, sir."

"Why, you see," explained the Justice, "Jay says Albion's been squatting on him, Mr. Ballister, every Sunday for six months. You see, Albion gets up when the choir sings, and watches 'em sharp to see they sing correct, because his ear ain't well tuned, but his eye's all right."

The Justice's round eyes blinked pleasantly. The court-room murmured with approval, and Albion started to his feet.

"Now don't interrupt the Court," continued the Justice. "You see, Mr. Ballister, sometimes Jay says it was a wasp and sometimes he says it was because Albion squatted on him, don't you see, bumped him on the ear with his elbow. You see, Jay sets just in front of Albion. Now, you see—"

"Then, does it not appear to your Honor that a witness who voluntarily offers to swear to two contradictory explanations; first, that the operation in question, the puncture or insertion, was performed by a wasp; secondly, that, though he did it himself with a pin and in his haste allowed that pin in damnatory evidence to remain, it was because, he alleges, of my client's posture toward, and intermittent contact with him—does it not seem to your Honor that such a witness is to be discredited in any statement he may make?"

"Well, really, Mr. Ballister, but you see Albion oughtn't to've squatted on him."

"I find myself in a singular position. It has not been usual in my experience to find the Court a pleader in opposition. I came hoping to inform and persuade your Honor regarding this case. I find myself in the position of being informed and persuaded. I hope the Court sees no discourtesy in the remark, but if the Court is prepared already to discuss the case there seems little for me to do."

The Justice looked alarmed. He felt his popularity trembling. It would not do to balk the public interest in Ballister's oratory. Doubtless Jay Dee had stuck a pin into Albion, but maybe Albion had mussed Jay's hair and jabbed his ear, had dragged and shaken him in the aisle at least. The rights of it did not seem difficult. They ought not to have acted that way. No man has the right to sit on another man's head from the standpoint or advantage of his own religious conviction. Nor has a man a right to use another man for a pincushion whenever, as it may be, he finds something about him in a way that's like a pincushion. But Ballister's oratory was critical and important.

"Why," said Kemegan hastily, "this Court is in a mighty uncertain state of mind. It couldn't make it up without hearing what you were going to say."

Again the Court murmured with approval. Ballister rose.

"This case presents singular features. The secret and sunless caverns, where human motives lie concealed, it is the function of justice to lay open to vivifying light. Not only evil or good intentions are moving forces of apparent action, but mistakes and misjudgments. I conclude that your Honor puts down the defendant's fanciful and predatory wasp to the defendant's neglect of legal advice, to his feeble and guilty ineptitude. I am willing to leave it there. I assume that he confesses the assault on my client's person with a pin, an insidious and lawless pin, pointed with cruelty and propelled with spite; I infer and understand that he offers in defence a certain alleged provocation, certain insertions of my client's elbow into the defendant's ear, certain trespasses and disturbance of the defendant's hair, finally, certain approximations and contacts between my client's adjacent quarter and the defendant's shoulders, denominated by him—and here we demur or object—as an act of sitting or squatting, whereby the defendant alleges himself to have been touched, grieved and annoyed. In the defendant's parsimonious neglect of counsel we generously supply him with a fair statement of his case. I return to my client.

"Your Honor, what nobler quality is there in our defective nature than that which enables the earnest man, whether as a citizen or in divine worship, whether in civil matters or religious, to abide steadfastly by his conscience and convictions. He stands a pillar of principle, a rock in the midst of uncertain waters. The feeble look up to him and are encouraged, the false and shifty are ashamed. His eye is fixed on the future. Posterity shall judge him. Small matters of his environment escape his notice. His mind is on higher things.

"I am not prepared to forecast the judgment of posterity on that point of ritualistic devotion to which my client is so devoted an advocate. Neither am I anxious or troubled to seek opinion whether my client inserted his elbow into the defendant's ear, or the defendant, maliciously or inadvertently, by some rotatory motion, applied, bumped or banged his ear against my client's elbow; whether the defendant rubbed or impinged with his head on the appendant coat tails of my client, or the reverse. I am uninterested in the alternative, indifferent to the whole matter. It seems to me an academic question. If the defendant so acted, it is not the action of which we complain. If my client once, twice, or even at sundry times, in his stern absorption, did not observe what may in casual accident have taken place behind, what then? I ask your Honor, what then? Did the defendant by a slight removal, by suggestion, by courteous remonstrance, attempt to obviate the difficulty? No! Did he remember those considerate virtues enjoined in Scripture, or the sacred place and ceremony in which he shared? No! Like a serpent, he coiled and waited. He hid his hypocrisy in white hairs, his venomous purpose in attitudes of reverence. He darkened his morbid malice till it festered, corroded, corrupted. He brooded over his fancied injury and developed his base design. Resolved and prepared, he watched his opportunity. With brazen and gangrened pin of malicious point and incensed propulsion, with averted eye and perfidious hand, with sudden, secret, backward thrust, with all the force of accumulated, diseased, despicable spite, he darted like a serpent's fang this misapplied instrument into the unprotected posterior, a sensitive portion, most outlying and exposed, of my client's person.

"This action, your Honor, I conceive to be in intent and performance a felonious, injurious and sufficient assault. For this injury, for pain, indignity and insult, for the vindication of justice in state and community, for the protection of the citizen from bold or treacherous attack, anterior or posterior, vanguard or rear, I ask your Honor that damages be given my client adequate to that injury, adequate to that vindication and protection."

So much and more Ballister spoke. Mr. Kernegan took off his spectacles and rubbed his forehead.

"Well," he said, "I guess Mr. Ballister'll charge Albion about forty dollars—"

Ballister started up.

"Don't interrupt the Court. It's worth all that. Albion and Jay haven't been acting right and they ought to pay for it between 'em. The Court decides Jay Dee shall pay twenty dollars damages and costs."

The court-room murmured with approval.

The twilight was gathering as Albion drove across the old covered bridge and turned into the road that leads to Ironville through a gloomy gorge of hemlock trees and low-browed rocks. The road keeps to the left above Diggory Brook, which murmurs in recesses below and waves little ghostly white garments over its waterfalls. Such is this murmur and the soft noise of the wind in the hemlocks, that the gorge is ever filled with a sound of low complaint. Twilight in the open sky is night below the hemlocks. At either end of the avenue you note where the light still glows fadingly. There lie the hopes and possibilities of a worldly day, skies, fields and market-places, to-days, to-morrows and yesterdays, and men walking about with confidence in their footing. But here the hemlocks stand beside in black order of pillars and whisper together distrustfully. The man who passes you is a nameless shadow with an intrusive, heavy footfall. Low voices float up from the pit of the gorge, intimations, regrets, discouragements, temptations.

A house and mill once stood at the lower end of it, and there, a century ago, was a wild crime done on a certain night; the dead bodies of the miller and his children lay on the floor, except one child, who hid and crept out in the grass; little trickles of blood stole along the cracks; house and mill blazed and fell down into darkness; a maniac cast his dripping axe into Diggory Brook and fled away yelling among the hills. Not that this had made the gorge any darker, or that its whispers are supposed to relate to any such memories. The brook comes from swamps and meadows like other brooks, and runs into the Pilgrim River. It is shallow and rapid, though several have contrived to fall and be drowned in it. One wonders how it could have happened. The old highway leading from Ramoth village to the valley has been grass-grown for generations, but that is because the other road is more direct to the Valley settlement and the station. The water of the brook is clear and pleasant enough. Much trillium, with its leaves like dark red splashes, a plant of sullen color and solitary station, used to grow there, but does so no more. Slender birches now creep down almost to the mouth of the gorge, and stand with white stems and shrinking, trembling leaves. But birches grow nearly everywhere.

Albion drove steadily up the darkened road, till his horse dropped into a walk behind an indistinguishable object that crept in front with creaking wheels. He shouted for passage and turned into the ditch on the side away from the gorge. The shadowy vehicle drifted slantingly aside. Albion started his horse; the front wheels of the two clicked, grated, slid inside each other and locked. Albion spoke impatiently. He was ever for quick decisions. He backed his horse, and the lock became hopeless. The unknown made no comment, no noise. The hemlocks whispered, the brook muttered in its pit and shook the little white garments of its waterfalls.

"Crank your wheel a trifle now."

The other did not move.

"Who are you? Can't ye speak?"

No answer.

Albion leaned over his wheel, felt the seat rail of the other vehicle, and brought his face close to something white—white hair about the approximate outline of a face. By the hair crossed by the falling hat brim, by the shoulders seen vaguely to be bent forward, by the loose creaking wheels of the buckboard he knew Jay Dee. The two stood close and breathless, face to face, but featureless and apart by the unmeasured distance of obscurity.

Albion felt a sudden uneasy thrill and drew back. He dreaded to hear Jay Dee's spiritless complaining voice, too much in the nature of that dusky, uncanny place. He felt as if something cold, damp and impalpable were drawing closer to him, whispering, calling his attention to the gorge, how black and steep! to the presence of Jay Dee, how near! to the close secret hemlocks covering the sky. This was not agreeable to a positive man, a man without fancies. Jay Dee sighed at last, softly, and spoke, piping, thin, half-moaning:

"You're following me. Let me alone!"

"I'm not following you," said Albion hoarsely. "Crank your wheel!"

"You're following me. I'm an old man. You're only fifty."

Albion breathed hard in the darkness. He did not understand either Jay Dee or himself. After a silence Jay Dee went on:

"I haven't any kin but you, Albion, except Stephen Ballister and the Winslows. They're only fourth cousins."

Albion growled.

"What do you mean?"

"Without my making a will it'd come to you, wouldn't it? Seems to me as if you oughtn't to pester me, being my nearest kin, and me, I ain't made any will. I got a little property, though it ain't much. 'Twould clear your mortgage and make you easy."

"What d'you mean?"

"Twenty dollars and costs," moaned Jay Dee. "And me an old man, getting ready for his latter end soon. I ain't made my will, either. I ought to've done it."

What could Jay Dee mean? If he made no will his property would come to Albion. No will made yet. A hinted intention to make one in favor of Stephen Ballister or the Winslows. The foundry was mortgaged.—Jay was worth sixty thousand. Diggory Gorge was a dark whispering place of ancient crime, of more than one unexplained accident. The hemlocks whispered, the brook gurgled and glimmered. Such darkness might well cloak and cover the sunny instincts that look upwards, scruples of the social daylight. Would Jay Dee trap him to his ruin? Jay Dee would not expect to enjoy it if he were dead himself. But accidents befall, and men not seldom meet sudden deaths, and an open, free-speaking neighbor is not suspected. Success lies before him in the broad road.

It rushed through Albion's mind, a flood, sudden, stupefying—thoughts that he could not master, push back, or stamp down.

He started and roused himself; his hands were cold and shaking. He sprang from his buggy and cried angrily:

"What d'ye mean by all that? Tempt me, a God-fearing man? Throw ye off'n the gorge! Break your old neck! I've good notion to it, if I wasn't a God-fearing man. Crank your wheel there!"

He jerked his buggy free, sprang in, and lashed his horse. The horse leaped, the wheels locked again. Jay Dee's buckboard, thrust slanting aside, went over the edge, slid and stopped with a thud, caught by the hemlock trunks. A ghostly glimmer of white hair one instant, and Jay Dee was gone down the black pit of the gorge. A wheezing moan, and nothing more was heard in the confusion. Then only the complaining murmur of the brook, the hemlocks at their secrets.

"Jay! Jay!" called Albion, and then leaped out, ran and whispered, "Jay!"

Only the mutter of the brook and the shimmer of foam could be made out as he stared and listened, leaning over, clinging to a tree, feeling about for the buckboard. He fumbled, lit a match and lifted it. The seat was empty, the left wheels still in the road. The two horses, with twisted necks and glimmering eyes, were looking back quietly at him, Albion Dee, a man of ideas and determination, now muttering things unintelligible in the same tone with the muttering water, with wet forehead and nerveless hands, heir of Jay Dee's thousands, staring down the gorge of Diggory Brook, the scene of old crime. He gripped with difficulty as he let himself slide past the first row of trees, and felt for some footing below. He noticed dully that it was a steep slope, not a precipice at that point. He lit more matches as he crept down, and peered around to find something crushed and huddled against some tree, a lifeless, fearful thing. The slope grew more moderate. There were thick ferns. And closely above the brook, that gurgled and laughed quietly, now near at hand, sat Jay Dee. He looked up and blinked dizzily, whispered and piped:

"Twenty dollars and costs! You oughtn't to pester me. I ain't made my will."

Albion sat down. They sat close together in the darkness some moments and were silent.

"You ain't hurt?" Albion asked at last. "We'll get out."

They went up the steep, groping and stumbling.

Albion half lifted his enemy into the buckboard, and led the horse, his own following. They were out into the now almost faded daylight. Jay sat holding his lines, bowed over, meek and venerable. The front of his coat was torn. Albion came to his wheel.

"Will twenty dollars make peace between you and me, Jay Dee?"

"The costs was ten," piping sadly.

"Thirty dollars, Jay Dee? Here it is."

He jumped into his buggy and drove rapidly. In sight of the foundry he drew a huge breath.

"I been a sinner and a fool," and slapped his knee. "It's sixty thousand dollars, maybe seventy. A self-righteous sinner and a cocksure fool. God forgive me!"

Between eight and nine Jay Dee sat down before his meagre fire and rusty stove, drank his weak tea and toasted his bread. The windows clicked with the night wind. The furniture was old, worn, unstable, except the large desk behind him full of pigeonholes and drawers. Now and then he turned and wrote on scraps of paper. Tea finished, he collected the scraps and copied:

Mr. Stephen Ballister: I feel, as growing somewhat old, I ought to make my will, and sometime, leaving this world for a better, would ask you to make my will for me, for which reasonable charge, putting this so it cannot be broken by lawyers, who will talk too much and are vain of themselves, that is, leaving all my property of all kinds to my relative, James Winslow of Wimberton, and not anything to Albion Dee; for he has not much sense but is hasty; for to look after the choir is not his business, and to sit on an old man and throw him from his own wagon and pay him thirty dollars is hasty, for it is not good sense, and not anything to Stephen Ballister, for he must be rich with talking so much in courts of this world. Put this all in my will, but if unable or unwilling on account of remorse for speaking so in the court, please to inform that I may get another lawyer. Yours,

Jay Dee.

He sealed and addressed the letter, put it in his pocket, and noticed the ruinous rent in his coat. He sighed, murmured over it complainingly, and turned up the lapel of the coat. Pins in great variety and number were there in careful order, some new, some small, some long and old and yellow. He selected four and pinned the rent together, sighing. Then he took three folded bills from his vest pocket, unfolded, counted and put them back, felt of the letter in his coat gently, murmured, "I had the best of Albion there; I had him there," took his candle and went up peacefully and venerably to bed.

A NIGHT'S LODGING

FATHER WILISTON was a retired clergyman, so distinguished from his son Timothy, whose house stood on the ridge north of the old village of Win-throp, and whose daily path lay between his house and the new growing settlement around the valley station. It occurred at odd times to Father Wiliston that Timothy's path was somewhat undeviating. The clergyman had walked widely since Win-throp was first left behind fifty-five years back, at a time when the town was smaller and cows cropped the Green but never a lawn mower.

After college and seminary had come the frontier, which lay this side of the Great Lakes until Clinton stretched his ribbon of waterway to the sea; then a mission in Wisconsin, intended to modify the restless profanity of lumbermen who broke legs under logs and drank disastrous whiskey. A city and twenty mills were on the spot now, though the same muddy river ran into the same blue lake. Some skidders and saw-tenders of old days were come to live in stone mansions and drive in nickel-plated carriages; some were dead; some drifting like the refuse on the lake front; some skidding and saw-tending still. Distinction of social position was an idea that Father Wiliston never was able to grasp.

In the memories of that raw city on the lake he had his place among its choicest incongruities; and when his threescore and ten years were full, the practical tenderness of his nickel-plated and mansioned parishioners packed him one day into an upholstered sleeping car, drew an astonishing check to his credit, and mailed it for safety to Timothy Wiliston of Winthrop. So Father Wiliston returned to Winthrop, where Timothy, his son, had been sent to take root thirty years before.

One advantage of single-mindedness is that life keeps on presenting us with surprises. Father Wiliston occupied his own Arcadia, and Wisconsin or Winthrop merely sent in to him a succession of persons and events of curious interest. "The parson"—Wisconsin so spoke of him, leaning sociably over its bar, or pausing among scented slabs and sawdust—"the parson resembles an egg as respects that it's innocent and some lopsided, but when you think he must be getting addled, he ain't. He says to me, 'You'll make the Lord a deal of trouble, bless my soul!' he says. I don't see how the Lord's going to arrange for you. But'—thinking he might hurt my feelings—'I guess he'll undertake it by and by.' Then he goes wabbling down-street, picks up Mike Riley, who's considerable drunk, and takes him to see his chickens. And Mike gets so interested in those chickens you'd like to die. Then parson goes off, absent-minded and forgets him, and Mike sleeps the balmy night in the barnyard, and steals a chicken in the morning, and parson says, 'Bless my soul! How singular!' Well," concluded Wisconsin, "he's getting pretty young for his years. I hear they're going to send him East before he learns bad habits."

The steadiness and repetition of Timothy's worldly career and semi-daily walk to and from his business therefore seemed to Father Wiliston phenomenal, a problem not to be solved by algebra, for if a equalled Timothy, b his house, c his business, $a + b + c$ was still not a far-reaching formula, and there seemed no advantage in squaring it. Geometrically it was evident that by walking back and forth over the same straight line you never so much as obtained an angle. Now, by arithmetic, "Four times thirty, multiplied by—leaving out Sundays—Bless me! How singular! Thirty-seven thousand five hundred and sixty times!"

He wondered if it had ever occurred to Timothy to walk it backward, or, perhaps, to hop, partly on one foot, and then, of course, partly on the other. Sixty years ago there was a method of progress known as "hop-skip-and-jump," which had variety and interest. Drawn in the train of this memory came other memories floating down the afternoon's slant sunbeams, rising from every meadow and clump of woods; from the elder swamp where the brown rabbits used to run zigzag, possibly still ran in the same interesting way; from the great sand bank beyond the Indian graves. The old Wiliston house, with roof that sloped like a well-sweep, lay yonder, a mile or two. He seemed to remember some one said it was empty, but he could not associate it with emptiness. The bough apples there, if he remembered rightly, were an efficacious balm for regret.

He sighed and took up his book. It was another cure for regret, a Scott novel, "The Pirate." It had points of superiority over Cruden's Concordance. The surf began to beat on the Shetland Islands, and trouble was imminent between Cleveland and Mor-daunt Mertoun.

Timothy and his wife drove away visiting that afternoon, not to return till late at night, and Bettina, the Scandinavian, laid Father Wiliston's supper by the open window, where he could look out across the porch and see the chickens clucking in the road.

"You mus' eat, fater," she commanded.

"Yes, yes, Bettina. Thank you, my dear. Quite right."

He came with his book and sat down at the table, but Bettina was experienced and not satisfied.

"You mus' eat firs'."

He sighed and laid down "The Pirate." Bettina captured and carried it to the other end of the room, lit the lamp though it was still light, and departed after the mail. It was a rare opportunity for her to linger in the company of one of her Scandinavian admirers. "Fater" would not know the difference between seven and nine or ten.

He leaned in the window and watched her safely out of sight, then went across the room, recaptured "The Pirate," and chuckled in the tickling pleasure of a forbidden thing, "asked the blessing," drank his tea shrewdly, knowing it would deteriorate, and settled to his book. The brown soft dusk settled, shade by shade; moths fluttered around the lamp; sleepy birds twittered in the maples. But the beat of the surf on the Shetland Islands was closer than these. Cleveland and Mordaunt Mertoun were busy, and Norna— "really, Norna was a remarkable woman"—and an hour slipped past.

Some one hemmed! close by and scraped his feet. It was a large man who stood there, dusty and ragged, one boot on the porch, with a red handkerchief knotted under his thick tangled beard and jovial red face. He had solid limbs and shoulders, and a stomach of sloth and heavy feeding.

The stranger did not resemble the comely pirate, Cleveland; his linen was not "seventeen hun'red;" it seemed doubtful if there were any linen. And yet, in a way there was something not inappropriate about him, a certain chaotic ease; not piratical, perhaps, although he looked like an adventurous person. Father Wiliston took time to pass from one conception of things to another. He gazed mildly through his glasses.

"I ain't had no supper," began the stranger in a deep moaning bass; and Father Wiliston started.

"Bless my soul! Neither have I." He shook out his napkin. "Bettina, you see "—

"Looks like there's enough for two," moaned and grumbled the other. He mounted the porch and approached the window, so that the lamplight glimmered against his big, red, oily face.

"Why, so there is!" cried Father Wiliston, looking about the table in surprise. "I never could eat all that. Come in." And the stranger rolled muttering and wheezing around through the door.

"Will you not bring a chair? And you might use the bread knife. These are fried eggs. And a little cold chicken? Really, I'm very glad you dropped in, Mr."—

"Del Toboso." By this time the stranger's mouth was full and his enunciation confused.

"Why"—Father Wiliston helped himself to an egg—"I don't think I caught the name."

"Del Toboso. Boozy's what they calls me in the push."

"I'm afraid your tea is quite cold. Boozy? How singular! I hope it doesn't imply alcoholic habits."

"No," shaking his head gravely, so that his beard wagged to the judicial negation. "Takes so much to tank me up I can't afford it, let alone it ain't moral."

The two ate with haste, the stranger from habit and experience, Father Wiliston for fear of Bettina's sudden return. When the last egg and slice of bread had disappeared, the stranger sat back with a wheezing sigh.

"I wonder," began Father Wiliston mildly, "Mr. Toboso—Toboso is the last name, isn't it, and Del the first?"

"Ah," the other wheezed mysteriously, "I don't know about that, Elder. That's always a question."

"You don't know! You don't know!"

"Got it off'n another man," went on Toboso sociably. "He said he wouldn't take fifty dollars for it. I didn't have no money nor him either, and he rolled off'n the top of the train that night or maybe the next I don't know. I didn't roll him. It was in Dakota, over a canyon with no special bottom. He scattered himself on the way down. But I says, if that name's worth fifty dollars, it's mine. Del Toboso. That's mine. Sounds valuable, don't it?"

Father Wiliston fell into a reverie. "To-boso? Why, yes. Dulcinea del Toboso. I remember, now."

"What's that? Dulcinea, was it? And you knowed him?"

"A long while ago when I was younger. It was in a green cover. 'Don Quixote'—he was in a cage, 'The Knight of the Rueful Countenance.' He had his face between the bars."

"Well," said Toboso, "you must have knowed him. He always looked glum, and I've seen him in quad myself."

"Yes. Sancho Panza. Dulcinea del Toboso."

"I never knowed that part of it. Dulcinea del Toboso! Well, that's me. You know a ruck of fine names, Elder. It sounds like thirteen trumps, now, don't it?"

Father Wiliston roused himself, and discriminated. "But you look more like Sancho Panza."

"Do? Well, I never knowed that one. Must've been a Greaser. Dulcinea's good enough."

Father Wiliston began to feel singularly happy and alive. The regular and even paced Timothy, his fidgeting wife, and the imperious Bettina were to some extent shadows and troubles in the evening of his life. They were careful people, who were hemmed in and restricted, who somehow hemmed in and restricted him. They lived up to precedents. Toboso did not seem to depend on precedents. He had the free speech, the casual inconsequence, the primitive mystery, desired of the boy's will and the wind's will, and travelled after by the long thoughts of youth. He was wind-beaten, burned red by the sun, ragged of coat and beard, huge, fat, wallowing in the ease of his flesh. One looked at him and remembered the wide world full of crossed trails and slumbering swamps.

Father Wiliston had long, straight white hair, falling beside his pale-veined and spiritual forehead and thin cheeks. He propped his forehead on one bony hand, and looked at Toboso with eyes of speculation. If both men were what some would call eccentric, to each other they seemed only companionable, which, after all, is the main thing.

"I have thought of late," continued Father Wiliston after a pause, "that I should like to travel, to examine human life, say, on the highway. I should think, now, your manner of living most interesting. You go from house to house, do you not?—from city to city? Like Ulysses, you see men and their labors, and you pass on. Like the apostles—who surely were wise men, besides that were especially maintained of God—like them, and the pilgrims to shrines, you go with wallet and staff or merely with Faith for your baggage."

"There don't nothing bother you in warm weather, that's right," said Toboso, "except your grub. And that ain't any more than's interesting. If it wasn't for looking after meals, a man on the road might get right down lazy."

"Why, just so! How wonderful! Now, do you suppose, Mr. Toboso, do you suppose it feasible? I should very much like, if it could be equably arranged, I should very much like to have this experience."

Toboso reflected. "There ain't many of your age on the road." An idea struck him suddenly. "But supposing you were going sort of experimenting, like that—and there's some folks that do—supposing you could lay your hands on a little bunch of money for luck, I don't see nothing to stop."

"Why, I think there is some in my desk." Toboso leaned forward and pulled his beard. The table creaked under his elbow. "How much?"

"I will see. Of course you are quite right."

"At your age, Elder."

"It is not as if I were younger."

Father Wiliston rose and hurried out.

Toboso sat still and blinked at the lamp. "My Gord!" he murmured and moaned confidentially, "here's a game!"

After some time Father Wiliston returned. "Do you think we could start now?" he asked eagerly.

"Why sure, Elder. What's hindering?"

"I am fortunate to find sixty dollars. Really, I didn't remember. And here's a note I have written to my son to explain. I wonder what Bettina did with my hat."

He hurried back into the hall. Toboso took the note from the table and pocketed it. "Ain't no use taking risks."

They went out into the warm night, under pleasant stars, and along the road together arm in arm.

"I feel pretty gay, Elder." He broke into bellowing song, "Hey, Jinny! Ho, Jinny! Listen, love, to me."

"Really, I feel cheerful, too, Mr. Toboso, wonderfully cheerful."

"Dulcinea, Elder. Dulcinea's me name. Hey, Jinny! Ho, Jinny!"

"How singular it is! I feel very cheerful. I think—really, I think I should like to learn that song about Jinny. It seems such a cheerful song."

"Hit her up, Elder," wheezed Toboso jovially. "Now then"—

"Hey, Jinny! Ho, Jinny! Listen, love, to me."

So they went arm in arm with a roaring and a tremulous piping.

The lamp flickered by the open window as the night breeze rose. Bettina came home betimes and cleared the table. The memory of a Scandinavian caress was too recent to leave room for her to remark that there were signs of devastating appetite, that dishes had been used unaccountably, and that "Fater" had gone somewhat early to bed. Timothy and his wife returned late. All windows and doors in the house of Timothy were closed, and the last lamp was extinguished.

Father Wiliston and Toboso went down the hill, silently, with furtive, lawless steps through the cluster of houses in the hollow, called Ironville, and followed then the road up the chattering hidden brook. The road came from the shadows of this gorge at last to meadows and wide glimmering skies, and joined the highway to Redfield. Presently they came to where a grassy side road slipped into the highway from the right, out of a land of bush and swamp and small forest trees of twenty or thirty years' growth. A large chestnut stood at the corner.

"Hey, Jinny!" wheezed Toboso. "Let's look at that tree, Elder."

"Look at it? Yes, yes. What for?" Toboso examined the bark by the dim starlight; Father Wiliston peered anxiously through his glasses to where Toboso's finger pointed.

"See those marks?"

"I'm afraid I don't. Really, I'm sorry."

"Feel 'em, then."

And Father Wiliston felt, with eager, excited finger.

"Them there mean there's lodging out here; empty house, likely."

"Do they, indeed. Very singular! Most interesting!" And they turned into the grassy road. The brushwood in places had grown close to it, though it seemed to be still used as a cart path. They came to a swamp, rank with mouldering vegetation, then to rising ground where once had been meadows, pastures, and plough lands.

Father Wiliston was aware of vaguely stirring memories. Four vast and aged maple trees stood close by the road, and their leaves whispered to the night; behind them, darkly, was a house with a far sloping roof in the rear. The windows were all glassless, all dark and dead-looking, except two in a front room, in which a wavering light from somewhere within trembled and cowered. They crept up, and looking through saw tattered wall paper and cracked plaster, and two men sitting on the floor, playing cards in the ghostly light of a fire of boards in the huge fireplace.

"Hey, Jinny!" roared Toboso, and the two jumped up with startled oaths. "Why, it's Boston Alley and the Newark Kid!" cried Toboso. "Come on, Elder."

The younger man cast forth zigzag flashes of blasphemy. "You big fat fool! Don't know no mor' 'n to jump like that on *me!* Holy Jims! I ain't made of copper."

Toboso led Father Wiliston round by the open door. "Hold your face, Kid. Gents, this here's a friend of mine we'll call the Elder, and let that go. I'm backing him, and I hold that goes. The Kid," he went on descriptively, addressing Father Wiliston, "is what you see afore you, Elder. His mouth is hot, his hands is cold, his nerves is shaky, he's always feeling the cops gripping his shirt-collar. He didn't see no clergy around. He begs your pardon. Don't he? I says, don't he?"

He laid a heavy red hand on the Newark Kid's shoulder, who wiped his pallid mouth with the back of his hand, smiled, and nodded.

Boston Alley seemed in his way an agreeable man. He was tall and slender limbed, with a long, thin black mustache, sinewy neck and hollow chest, and spoke gently with a sweet, resonant voice, saying, "Glad to see you, Elder."

These two wore better clothes than Toboso, but he seemed to dominate them with his red health and windy voice, his stomach and feet, and solidity of standing on the earth.

Father Wiliston stood the while gazing vaguely through his spectacles. The sense of happy freedom and congenial companionship that had been with him during the starlit walk had given way gradually to a stream of confused memories, and now these memories stood ranged about, looking at him with sad, faded eyes, asking him to explain the scene. The language of the Newark Kid had gone by him like a white hot blast. The past and present seemed to have about the same proportions of vision and reality. He could not explain them to each other. He looked up to Toboso, pathetically, trusting in his help.

"It was my house."

Toboso stared surprised. "I ain't on to you, Elder."

"I was born here."

Indeed Toboso was a tower of strength even against the ghosts of other days, reproachful for their long durance in oblivion.

"Oh! Well, by Jinny! I reckon you'll give us lodging, Elder," he puffed cheerfully. He took the coincidence so pleasantly and naturally that Father Wiliston was comforted, and thought that after all it was pleasant and natural enough.

The only furniture in the room was a high-backed settle and an overturned kitchen table, with one leg gone, and the other three helplessly in the air—so it had lain possibly many years. Boston Alley drew forward the settle and threw more broken clapboards on the fire, which blazed up and filled the room with flickering cheer. Soon the three outcasts were smoking their pipes and the conversation became animated.

"When I was a boy," said Father Wiliston—"I remember so distinctly—there were remarkable early bough apples growing in the orchard."

"The pot's yours, Elder," thundered To-boso. They went out groping under the old apple trees, and returned laden with plump pale green fruit. Boston Alley and the Newark Kid stretched themselves on the floor on heaps of pulled grass. Toboso and Father Wiliston sat on the settle. The juice of the bough apples ran with a sweet tang. The palate rejoiced and the soul responded. The Newark Kid did swift, cunning card tricks that filled Father Wiliston with wonder and pleasure.

"My dear young man, I don't see how you do it!"

The Kid was lately out of prison from a two years' sentence, "only for getting into a house by the window instead of the door," as Boston Alley delicately explained, and the "flies," meaning officers of the law, "are after him again for reasons he ain't quite sure of." The pallor of slum birth and breeding, and the additional prison pallor, made his skin look curious where the grime had not darkened it. He had a short-jawed, smooth-shaven face, a flat mouth and light hair, and was short and stocky, but lithe and noiseless in movement, and inclined to say little. Boston Alley was a man of some slight education, who now sometimes sung in winter variety shows, such songs as he picked up here and there in summer wanderings, for in warm weather he liked footing the road better, partly because the green country sights were pleasant to him, and partly because he was irresolute and keeping engagements was a distress. He seemed agreeable and sympathetic.

"He ain't got no more real feelings 'n a fish," said Toboso, gazing candidly at Boston, but speaking to Father Wiliston, "and yet he looks like he had 'em, and a man's glad to see him. Ain't seen you since fall, Boston, but I see the Kid last week at a hang-out in Albany. Well, gents, this ain't a bad lay."

Toboso himself had been many years on the road. He was in a way a man of much force and decision, and probably it was another element in him, craving sloth and easy feeding, which kept him in this submerged society; although here, too, there seemed room for the exercise of his dominance. He leaned back in the settle, and had his hand on Father Wiliston's shoulder. His face gleamed redly over his bison beard.

"It's a good lay. And we're gay, Elder. Ain't we gay? Hey, Jinny!"

"Yes, yes, Toboso. But this young man—I'm sure he must have great talents, great talents, quite remarkable. Ah—yes, Jinny!"

"Hey, Jinny," they sang together, "Ho, Jinny! Listen, love, to me. I'll sing to you, and play to you, a dulcet melode-e-e"—while Boston danced a shuffle and the Kid snapped the cards in time. Then, at Toboso's invitation and command, Boston sang a song, called "The Cheerful Man," resembling a ballad, to a somewhat monotonous tune, and perhaps known in the music halls of the time—all with a sweet, resonant voice and a certain pathos of intonation:—

"I knew a man across this land

Came waving of a cheerful hand,
Who drew a gun and gave some one
A violent contus-i-on,
This cheerful man.

"They sent him up, he fled from 'quad'
By a window and the grace of God,
Picked up a wife and children six,
And wandered into politics,
This cheerful man.

"'In politics he was, I hear,
A secret, subtle financier—
So the jury says, 'But we agree
He quits this sad community,
This cheerful man.'

"His wife and six went on the town,
And he went off; without a frown
Reproaching Providence, went he
And got another wife and three,
This cheerful man.

"He runs a cross-town car to-day
From Bleecker Street to Avenue A.
He swipes the fares with skilful ease,
Keeps up his hope, and tries to please,
This cheerful man.

"Our life is mingled woe and bliss,

Man that is born of woman is

Short-lived and goes to his long home.

Take heart, and learn a lesson from

This cheerful man."

"But," said Father Wiliston, "don't you think really, Mr. Alley, that the moral is a little confused? I don't mean intentionally," he added, with anxious precaution, "but don't you think he should have reflected"—

"You're right, Elder," said Toboso, with decision. "It's like that. It ain't moral. When a thing ain't moral that settles it." And Boston nodded and looked sympathetic with every one.

"I was sure you would agree with me," said Father Wiliston. He felt himself growing weary now and heavy-eyed. Presently somehow he was leaning on Toboso with his head on his shoulder. Toboso's arm was around him, and Toboso began to hum in a kind of wheezing lullaby, "Hey, Jinny! Ho, Jinny!"

"I am very grateful, my dear friends," murmured Father Wiliston. "I have lived a long time. I fear I have not always been careful in my course, and am often forgetful. I think"—drowsily—"I think that happiness must in itself be pleasing to God. I was often happy before in this room. I remember—my dear mother sat here—who is now dead. We have been quite, really quite cheerful to-night. My mother—was very judicious—an excellent wise woman—she died long ago." So he was asleep before any one was aware, while Toboso crooned huskily, "Hey, Jinny!" and Boston Alley and the Newark Kid sat upright and stared curiously.

"Holy Jims!" said the Kid.

Toboso motioned them to bring the pulled grass. They piled it on the settle, let Father Wiliston down softly, brought the broken table, and placed it so that he could not roll off.

"Well," said Toboso, after a moment's silence, "I guess we'd better pick him and be off. He's got sixty in his pocket."

"Oh," said Boston, "that's it, is it?"

"It's my find, but seeing you's here I takes half and give you fifteen apiece."

"Well, that's right."

"And I guess the Kid can take it out."

The Kid found the pocketbook with sensitive gliding fingers, and pulled it out. Toboso counted and divided the bills.

"Well," whispered Toboso thoughtfully, "if the Elder now was forty years younger, I wouldn't want a better pardner." They tiptoed out into the night. "But," he continued, "looking at it that way, o' course he ain't got no great use for his wad and won't remember it till next week. Heeled all right, anyhow. Only, I says now, I says, there ain't no vice in him."

"Mammy tuck me up, no licks to-night," said the Kid, plodding in front. "I ain't got nothing against him."

Boston Alley only fingered the bills in his pocket.

It grew quite dark in the room they had left as the fire sunk to a few flames, then to dull embers and an occasional darting spark. The only sound was Father Wiliston's light breathing.

When he awoke the morning was dim in the windows. He lay a moment confused in mind, then sat up and looked around.

"Dear me! Well, well, I dare say Toboso thought I was too old. I dare say"—getting on his feet—"I dare say they thought it would be unkind to tell me so."

He wandered through the dusky old rooms and up and down the creaking stairs, picking up bits of recollection, some vivid, some more dim than the dawn, some full of laughter, some that were leaden and sad; then out into the orchard to find a bough apple in the dewy grasses; and, kneeling under the gnarled old tree to make his morning prayer, which included in petition the three overnight revellers, he went in fluent phrase and broken tones among eldest memories.

He pushed cheerfully into the grassy road now, munching his apple and humming, "Hey, Jinny! Ho, Jinny!" He examined the tree at the highway with fresh interest. "How singular! It means an empty house. Very intelligent man, Toboso."

Bits of grass were stuck on his back and a bramble dragged from his coat tail. He plodded along in the dust and wabbled absent-mindedly from one side of the road to the other. The dawn towered behind him in purple and crimson, lifted its robe and canopy, and flung some kind of glittering gauze far beyond him. He did not notice it till he reached the top of the hill above Ironville with Timothy's house in sight. Then he stopped, turned, and was startled a moment; then smiled companionably on the state and glory of the morning, much as on Toboso and the card tricks of the Newark Kid.

"Really," he murmured, "I have had a very good time."

He met Timothy in the hall.

"Been out to walk early, father? Wait—there's grass and sticks on your coat."

It suddenly seemed difficult to explain the entire circumstances to Timothy, a settled man and girt with precedent.

"Did you enjoy it?—Letter you dropped? No, I haven't seen it. Breakfast is ready."

Neither Bettina nor Mrs. Timothy had seen the letter.

"No matter, my dear, no matter. I—really, I've had a very good time."

Afterward he came out on the porch with his Bible and Concordance, sat down and heard Bettina brushing his hat and ejaculating, "Fater!" Presently he began to nod drowsily and his head dropped low over the Concordance. The chickens clucked drowsily in the road.

———————————

ON EDOM HILL

I.

CHARLIE SEBASTIAN was a turfman, meaning that he had something to do with race-horses, and knew property as rolls of bank bills, of which one now and then suddenly has none at all; or as pacers and trotters that are given to breaking and unaccountably to falling off in their nervous systems; or as "Association Shares" and partnership investments in a training stable; all capable of melting and going down in one vortex. So it happened at the October races. And from this it arose that in going between two heated cities and low by the sea he stopped among the high hills that were cold.

He was a tall man with a pointed beard, strong of shoulder and foot, and without fear in his eyes. After two hours' riding he woke from a doze and argued once more that he was a "phenomenally busted man." It made no difference, after all, which city he was in. Looking out at the white hills that showed faintly in the storm, it occurred to him that this was not the railway line one usually travelled to the end in view. It was singular, the little difference between choices. You back the wrong horse; then you drink beer instead of fizz, and the results of either are tolerable. Let a man live lustily and there's little to regret. He had found ruin digestible before, and never yet gone to the dogs that wait to devour human remnants, but had gotten up and fallen again, and on the whole rejoiced. Stomach and lungs of iron, a torrent of red blood in vein and artery maintain their consolations; hopes rise again, blunders and evil doings seem to be practically outlived. So without theory ran Sebastian's experience. The theory used to be that his sin would find a man out. There were enough of Sebastian's that had gone out, and never returned to look for him. So too with mistakes and failures. A little while, a year or more, and you are busy with other matters. It is a stirring world, and offers no occupation for ghosts. The dragging sense of depression that he felt seemed natural enough; not to be argued down, but thrown aside in due time. Yet it was a feeling of pallid and cold futility, like the spectral hills and wavering snow.

"I might as well go back!"

He tossed a coin to see whether it was fated he should drop off at the next station, and it was.

"Ramoth!" cried the brakeman.

Sebastian held in his surprise as a matter of habit.

But on the platform in the drift and float of the snow-storm he stared around at the white January valley, at the disappearing train, at the sign above the station door, "Ramoth."

"That's the place," he remarked. "There wasn't any railroad then."

There were hidden virtues in a flipped coin. Sebastian had his superstitions.

The road to Ramoth village from the station curves about to the south of the great bare dome that is called Edom Hill, but Sebastian, without inquiry, took the fork to the left which climbed up the hill without compromise, and seemed to be little used.

Yet in past times Edom Hill was noted in a small way as a hill that upheld the house of a stern abolitionist, and in a more secret way as a station in the "underground railroad," or system by which runaway slaves were passed on to Canada. But when Charlie Sebastian remembered his father and Edom Hill, the days of those activities were passed. The abolitionist had nothing to exercise resistance and aggression on but his wind-blown farm and a boy, who was aggressive to seek out mainly the joys of this world, and had faculties of resistance. There were bitter clashes; young Sebastian fled, and came upon a stable on a stud farm, and from there in due time went far and wide, and found tolerance in time and wrote, offering to "trade grudges and come to see how he was."

The answer, in a small, faint, cramped, unskilful hand, stated the abolitionist's death. "Won't you come back, Mr. Sebastian. It is lonely. Harriet Sebastian." And therefore Sebastian remarked:

"You bet it is! Who's she? The old man must have married again."

In his new-found worldly tolerance he had admired such aggressive enterprise, but seeing no interest in the subject, had gone his way and forgotten it.

Beating up Edom Hill through the snow was no easier than twenty years before. David Sebastian had built his house in a high place, and looking widely over the top of the land, saw that it was evil.

The drifts were unbroken and lay in long barrows and windy ridges over the roadway. The half-buried fences went parallel up the white breast and barren heave of the hill, and disappeared in the storm. Sebastian passed a house with closed blinds, then at a long interval a barn and a stiff red chimney with a snow-covered heap of ruins at its foot. The station was now some miles behind and the dusk was coming on. The broad top of the hill was smooth and rounded gradually. Brambles, bushes, reeds, and the tops of fences broke the surface of the snow, and beside these only a house by the road, looking dingy and gray, with a blackish barn attached, four old maples in front, an orchard behind. Far down the hill to the right lay the road to Ramoth, too far for its line of naked trees to be seen in the storm. The house on Edom

Hill had its white throne to itself, and whatever dignity there might be in solitude.

He did not pause to examine the house, only noticed the faint smoke in one chimney, opened the gate, and pushed through untrodden snow to the side door and knocked. The woman who came and stood in the door surprised him even more than "Ramoth!" called by the brakeman. Without great reason for seeming remarkable, it seemed remarkable. He stepped back and stared, and the two, looking at each other, said nothing. Sebastian recovered.

"My feet are cold," he said slowly. "I shouldn't like to freeze them."

She drew back and let him in, left him to find a chair and put his feet against the stove. She sat down near the window and went on knitting. The knitting needles glittered and clicked. Her face was outlined against the gray window, the flakes too glittered and clicked. It looked silent, secret, repressed, as seen against the gray window; like something chilled and snowed under, cold and sweet, smooth pale hair and forehead, deep bosom and slender waist. She looked young enough to be called in the early June of her years.

"There's good proportion and feature, but not enough nerves for a thoroughbred. But," he thought, "she looks as if she needed, as you might say, revelry," and he spoke aloud.

"Once I was in this section and there was a man named Sebastian lived here, or maybe it was farther on."

She said, "It was here" in a low voice.

"David Sebastian now, that was it, or something that way. Stiff, sort of grim old—oh, but you might be a relative, you see. Likely enough. So you might."

"I might be."

"Just so. You might be."

He rubbed his hands and leaned back, staring at the window. The wind was rising outside and blew the snow in whirls and sheets.

"Going to be a bad night I came up from the station. If a man's going anywhere tonight, he'll be apt not to get there."

"You ought to have taken the right hand at the fork."

"Well, I don't know."

She rose and took a cloak from the table. Sebastian watched her.

"I must feed the pony and shut up the chickens."

She hesitated. A refusal seemed to have been hinted to the hinted request for hospitality. But Sebastian saw another point.

"Now, that's what I'm going to do for you."

She looked on silently, as he passed her with assured step, not hesitating at doors, but through the kitchen to the woodshed, and there in the darkness of a pitch-black corner took down a jingling lantern and lit it. She followed him silently into the yard, that was full of drifts and wild storm, to the barn, where she listened to him shake down hay and bedding, measure oats, slap the pony's flank and chirp cheerfully. Then he plunged through a low door and she heard the bolt in the chicken shed rattle. It had grown dark outside. He came out and held the barn door, waiting for her to step out, and they stood side by side on the edge of the storm.

"How did you know the lantern was there?"

"Lantern! Oh, farmhouses always keep the lantern in the nearest corner of the woodshed, if it isn't behind the kitchen door."

But she did not move to let him close the bam. He looked down at her a moment and then out at the white raging night.

"Can't see forty feet, can you? But, of course, if you don't want to give me a roof I'll have to take my chances. Look poor, don't they? Going to let me shut this door?"

"I am quite alone here."

"So am I. That's the trouble."

"I don't think you understand," she said quietly, speaking in a manner low, cool, and self-contained.

"I've got more understanding now than I'll have in an hour, maybe."

"I will lend you the lantern."

"Oh, you mightn't get it back." He drew the barn door to, which forced her to step forward. A gust of wind about the corner of the bam staggered and threw her back. He caught her about her shoulders and held her steadily, and shot the bolt with the hand that held the lantern.

"That's all right. A man has to take his chances. I dare say a woman had better not."

If Sebastian exaggerated the dangers of the night, if there were any for him, looked at from her standpoint they might seem large and full of dread. The wind howled with wild hunting sound, and shrieked against the eaves of the house. The snow drove thick and blinding. The chimneys were invisible. A woman easily transfers her own feelings to a man and interprets them there. In the interest of that interpretation it might no longer seem possible that man's ingratitude, or his failings and passions, could be as unkind as winter wind and bitter sky.

She caught her breath in a moment.

"You will stay to supper," she said, and stepped aside.

"No. As I'm going, I'd better go."

She went before him across the yard, opened the woodshed door and stood in it. He held out the lantern, but she did not take it. He lifted it to look at her face, and she smiled faintly.

"Please come in."

"Better go on, if I'm going. Am I?"

"I'm very cold. Please come in."

They went in and closed the doors against the storm. The house was wrapped round, and shut away from the sight of Edom Hill, and Edom Hill was wrapped round and shut away from the rest of the world.

II.

Revelry has need of a certain co-operation. Sebastian drew heavily on his memory for entertainment, told of the combination that had "cleaned him out," and how he might get in again in the Spring, only he felt a bit tired in mind now, and things seemed dead. He explained the mysteries of "short prices, selling allowances, past choices, hurdles and handicaps," and told of the great October races, where Decatur won from Clifford and Lady Mary, and Lady Mary ran through the fence and destroyed the features of the jockey. But the quiet, smooth-haired woman maintained her calm, and offered neither question nor comment, only smiled and flushed faintly now and then. She seemed as little stirred by new tumultuous things as the white curtains at the windows, that moved slightly when the storm, which danced and shouted on Edom Hill, managed to force a whistling breath through a chink.

Sebastian decided she was frozen up with loneliness and the like. "She's got no conversation, let alone revelry." He thought he knew what her life was like. "She's sort of empty. Nothing doing any time. It's the off season all the year. No troubles. Sort of like a fish, as being chilly and calm, that lives in cold water till you have to put pepper on to taste it. I know how it goes on this old hill."

She left him soon. He heard her moving about in the kitchen, and sometimes the clink of a dish. He sat by the stove and mused and muttered. She came and told him his room was on the left of the stair; it had a stove; would he not carry up wood and have his fire there? She seemed to imply a preference that he should. But the burden and oppression of his musings kept him from wondering when she had compromised her scruples and fears, or why she kept any of them. He mounted the stair with his wood. She followed with a lamp and left him. He stared at the closed door and rubbed his chin thoughtfully, then went to work with his fire. The house became silent, except for the outer tumult. She did not mount the stair again; it followed that she slept below.

Sebastian took a daguerreotype from the mantel and stared at it. It was the likeness of a shaven, grim-faced man in early middle life. He examined it long with a quizzical frown; finally went to the washstand, opened the drawer and took out a razor with a handle of yellow bone, carried the washstand to the stove, balanced the mirror against the pitcher, stropped the razor on his hand, heated water in a cup, slowly dismantled his face of beard and mustache, cast them in the stove, put the daguerreotype beside the mirror, and compared critically. Except that the face in the daguerreotype had a straight, set mouth, and the face in the mirror was one full-lipped and humorous and differently lined, they were nearly the same.

"I wouldn't have believed it"

He put it aside and looked around, whistling in meditation. Then he went back again to wondering who the pale-haired woman was. Probably the farm had changed hands. A man whose father had been dead going on twenty years couldn't have that kind of widowed stepmother. He was disqualified.

A cold, unchanging place, Edom Hill, lifted out of the warm, sapping currents of life. It might be a woman could keep indefinitely there, looking much the same. If her pulse beat once to an ordinary twice, she ought to last twice as long. The house seemed unchanged. The old things were in their old familiar places, David Sebastian's books on their shelves in the room below, on the side table there his great Bible, in which he used to write all family records, with those of his reforming activity. Sebastian wondered what record stood of his own flight.

He sat a few moments longer, then took his lamp and crept softly out of the room and down the stairs. The sitting-room was icily cold now; the white curtains stirred noiselessly. He sat down before the little side table and opened the great book.

There were some thirty leaves between the Old and New Testaments, most of them stitched in. A few at the end were blank. Some of the records were obscure.

"March 5th, 1840. Saw light on this subject."

Others ran:

"Sept. 1 st, 1843. Rec. Peter Cavendish, fugitive."

"Dec. 3d, ditto. Rec. Robert Henry."

"April 15th, ditto. Rec. one, Æsop," and so on.

"Dec. 14th, 1848. Have had consolation from prayer for public evil."

"April 20th, 1858. My son, Charles Sebastian, born."

"April 7th, 1862. My wife, Jane Sebastian, died."

"July 5th, 1862. Rec. Keziah Andrews to keep my house."

The dates of the entries from that point grew further apart, random and obscure; here and there a fact.

"Nov. 4th, 1876. Charles Sebastian departed."

"June 9th, 1877. Rec. Harriet."

"Jan. 19th, 1880. Have wrestled in prayer without consolation for Charles Sebastian."

This was the last entry. A faint line ran down across the page connecting the end of "Harriet" with the beginning of "Charles." Between the two blank leaves at the end was a photograph of himself at seventeen. He remembered suddenly how it was taken by a travelling photographer, who had stirred his soul with curiosity and given him the picture; and David Sebastian had taken it and silently put it away among blank leaves of the Bible.

Sebastian shivered. The written leaves, the look of himself of twenty years before, the cold, the wail of the wind, the clicking flakes on the window panes, these seemed now to be the dominant facts of life. Narrow was it, poor and meagre, to live and labor with a barren farm? The old abolitionist had cut deeper into existence than he had. If to deal with the fate of races, and wrestle alone with God on Edom Hill, were not knowledge and experience, what was knowledge or experience, or what should a man call worth the trial of his brain and nerve?

"He passed me. He won hands down," he muttered, bending over the page again. "'Rec. Harriet.' That's too much for me." And he heard a quick noise behind him and turned.

She stood in the door, wide-eyed, smooth, pale hair falling over one shoulder, long cloak half slipped from the other, holding a shotgun, threatening and stem.

"What are you doing here?"

"Out gunning for me?" asked Sebastian gravely.

She stared wildly, put the gun down, cried:

"You're Charlie Sebastian!" and fell on her knees beside the stove, choking, sobbing and shaking, crouching against the cold sheet iron in a kind of blind memory of its warmth and protection.

"You still have the drop on me," said Sebastian.

She shivered and crouched still and whispered:

"I'm cold."

"How long have you been here freezing?"

Sebastian thrust anything inflammable at hand into the stove, lit it and piled in the wood.

"Not long. Only—only a few moments."

"You still have the advantage of me. Who are you?"

"Why, I'm Harriet," she said simply, and looked up.

"Just so. 'Received, 1877.' How old were you then?"

"Why, I was eight."

"Just so. Don't tell lies, Harriet. You've been freezing a long while."

She drew her cloak closer over the thin white linen of her gown with shaking hand.

"I don't understand. I'm very cold. Why didn't you come before? It has been so long waiting."

III.

The draft began to roar and the dampers to glow. She crept in front of the glow. He drew a chair and sat down close behind her.

"Why didn't you come before?"

The question was startling, for Sebastian was only conscious of a lack of reason for coming. If David Sebastian had left him the farm he would have heard from it, and being prosperous, he had not cared. But the question seemed to imply some strong assumption and further knowledge.

"You'd better tell me about it."

"About what? At the beginning?"

"Aren't you anything except 'Received, Harriet'?"

"Oh, I hadn't any father or mother when Mr. Sebastian brought me here. Is that what you mean? But he taught me to say 'Harriet Sebastian,' and a great many things he taught me. Didn't you know? And about his life and what he wanted you to do? Because, of course, we talked about you nearly always in the time just before he died. He said you would be sure to come, but he died, don't you see? only a few years after, and that disappointed him. He gave me the picture and said, 'He'll come, and you'll know him by this,' and he said, 'He will come poor and miserable. My only son, so I leave him to you; and so, as I did, you will pray for him twice each day.' It was just like that, 'Tell Charles there is no happiness but in duty. Tell him I found it so.' It was a night like this when he died, and Kezzy was asleep in her chair out here, and I sat by the bed. Then he told me I would pay him all in that way by doing what he meant to do for you. I was so little, but I seemed to understand that I was to live for it, as he had lived to help free the slaves. Don't you see? Then he began calling, 'Charles! Charles!' as if you were somewhere near, and I fell asleep, and woke and lay still and listened to the wind; and when I tried to get up I couldn't, because he held my hair, and he was dead. But why didn't you come?"

"It looks odd enough now," Sebastian admitted, and wondered at the change from still impassiveness, pale and cool silence, to eager speech, swift question, lifted and flushed face.

"Then you remember the letters? But you didn't come then. But I began to fancy how it would be when you came, and then somehow it seemed as if you were here. Out in the orchard sometimes, don't you see? And more often when Kezzy was cross. And when she went to sleep by the fire at night—she was so old—we were quite alone and talked. Don't you remember?—I mean—But Kezzy didn't like to hear me talking to myself. 'Mutter, mutter!' like that. 'Never was such a child!' And then she died, too, seven—seven years ago, and it was quite different. I—I grew older. You seemed to be here quite and quite close to me always. There was no one else, except—But, I don't know why, I had an aching from having to wait, and it has been a long time, hasn't it?"

"Rather long. Go on. There was no one else?"

"No. We lived here—I mean—it grew that way, and you changed from the picture, too, and became like Mr. Sebastian, only younger, and just as you are now, only—not quite."

She looked at him with sudden fear, then dropped her eyes, drew her long hair around under her cloak and leaned closer to the fire.

"But there is so much to tell you it comes out all mixed."

Sebastian sat silently looking down at her, and felt the burden of his thinking grow heavier; the pondering how David Sebastian had left him an inheritance of advice, declaring his own life full and brimming, and to Harriet the inheritance of a curious duty that had grown to people her nights and days with intense sheltered dreams, and made her life, too, seem to her full and brimming, multitudinous with events and interchanges, himself so close and cherished an actor in it that his own parallel unconsciousness of it had almost dropped out of conception. And the burden grew heavier still with the weight of memories, and the record between the Old and New Testaments; with the sense of the isolation and covert of the midnight, and the storm; with the sight of Harriet crouching by the fire, her story, how David Sebastian left this world and went out into the wild night crying, "Charles! Charles!" It was something not logical, but compelling. It forced him to remark that his own cup appeared partially empty from this point of view. Harriet seemed to feel that her hour had come and he was given to her hands.. Success even in methods of living is a convincing thing over unsuccess. Ah, well! too late to remodel to David Sebastian's notion. It was singular, though, a woman silent, restrained, scrupulous, moving probably to the dictates of village opinion— suddenly the key was turned, and she threw back the gates of her prison; threw open doors, windows, intimate curtains; asked him to look in and explore everywhere and know all the history and the forecasts; became simple, primitive, unrestrained, willing to sit there at his feet and as innocent as her white linen gown. How smooth and pale her hair was and gentle cheek, and there were little sleepy smiles in the corners of the lips. He thought he would like most of all to put out his hand and touch her cheek and sleepy smiles, and draw her hair, long and soft and pale, from under the cloak. On the whole, it seemed probable that he might.

"Harriet," he said slowly, "I'm going to play this hand."

"Why, I don't know what you mean."

"Take it, I'm not over and above a choice selection. I don't mention details, but take it as a general fact. Would you want to marry that kind of a selection, meaning me?"

"Oh, yes! Didn't you come for that? I thought you would."

"And I thought you needed revelry! You must have had a lot of it."

"I don't know what you mean. Listen! It keeps knocking at the door!"

"Oh, that's all right. Let it knock. Do you expect any more vagrants?"

"Vagrants?"

"Like me."

"Like you? You only came home. Listen! It was like this when he died. But he wouldn't come to-night and stand outside and knock, would he? Not to-night, when you've come at last. But he used to. Of course, I fancied things. It's the storm. There's no one else now."

A thousand spectres go whirling across Edom Hill such winter nights and come with importunate messages, but if the door is close and the fire courageous, it matters little. They are but wind and drift and out in the dark, and if one is in the light, it is a great point to keep the door fast against them and all forebodings, and let the coming days be what they will.

Men are not born in a night, or a year.

But if David Sebastian were a spectre there at the door, and thought differently on any question, or had more to say, he was not articulate. There is no occupation for ghosts in a stirring world, nor efficiency in their repentance.

Has any one more than a measure of hope, and a door against the storm? There was that much, at least, on Edom Hill.

———

SONS OF R. RAND

SOME years ago, of a summer afternoon, a perspiring organ-grinder and a leathery ape plodded along the road that goes between thin-soiled hillsides and the lake which is known as Elbow Lake and lies to the northeast of the village of Salem. In those days it was a well-travelled highway, as could be seen from its breadth and' dustiness. At about half the length of its bordering on the lake there was a spring set in the hillside, and a little pool continually rippled by its inflow. Some settler or later owner of the thin-soiled hillsides had left a clump of trees about it, making as sightly and refreshing an Institute of Charity as could be found. Another philanthropist had added half a cocoanut-shell to the foundation.

The organ-grinder turned in under the trees with a smile, in which his front teeth played a large part, and suddenly drew back with a guttural exclamation; the leathery ape bumped against his legs, and both assumed attitudes expressing respectively, in an Italian and tropical manner, great surprise and abandonment of ideas. A tall man lay stretched on his back beside the spring, with a felt hat over his face. Pietro, the grinder, hesitated. The American, if disturbed and irascible, takes by the collar and kicks with the foot: it has sometimes so happened. The tall man pushed back his hat and sat up, showing a large-boned and sun-browned face, shaven except for a black mustache, clipped close. He looked not irascible, though grave perhaps, at least unsmiling. He said: "It's free quarters, Dago. Come in. Entrez. Have a drink."

Pietro bowed and gesticulated with amiable violence. "Dry!" he said. "Oh, hot!"

"Just so. That a friend of yours?"—pointing to the ape. "He ain't got a withering sorrow, has he? Take a seat."

Elbow Lake is shaped as its name implies. If one were to imagine the arm to which the elbow belonged, it would be the arm of a muscular person in the act of smiting a peaceable-looking farmhouse a quarter of a mile to the east. Considering the bouldered front of the hill behind the house, the imaginary blow would be bad for the imaginary knuckles. It is a large house, with brown, unlikely looking hillsides around it, huckleberry knobs and ice-grooved boulders here and there. The land between it and the lake is low, and was swampy forty years ago, before the Rand boys began to drain it, about the time when R. Rand entered the third quarter century of his unpleasant existence.

R. Rand was, I suppose, a miser, if the term does not imply too definite a type. The New England miser is seldom grotesque. He seems more like congealed than distorted humanity. He does not pinch a penny so hard as some of other races are said to do, but he pinches a dollar harder, and is quite as unlovely as any. R. Rand's methods of obtaining dollars to pinch were not altogether known, or not, at least, recorded—which accounts perhaps for the tradition that they were of doubtful uprightness. He held various mortgages about the county, and his farm represented little to him except a means of keeping his two sons inexpensively employed in rooting out stones.

At the respective ages of sixteen and seventeen the two sons, Bob and Tom Rand, discovered the rooting out of stones to be unproductive labor, if nothing grew, or was expected to grow, in their place, except more stones; and the nature of the counsels they took may be accurately imagined. In the autumn of '56 they began ditching the swamp in the direction of the lake, and in the summer of '57 raised a crop of tobacco in the northeast corner, R. Rand, the father, making no comment the while. At the proper time he sold the tobacco to Packard & Co., cigar makers, of the city of Hamilton, still making no comment, probably enjoying some mental titillation. Tom Rand then flung a rock of the size of his fist through one of the front windows, and ran away, also making no comment further than that. The broken window remained broken twenty-five years, Tom returning neither to mend it nor to break another. Bob Rand, by some bargain with his father, continued the ditching and planting of the swamp with some profit to himself.

He evidently classed at least a portion of his father's manner of life among the things that are to be avoided. He acquired a family, and was in the way to bring it up in a reputable way. He further cultivated and bulwarked his reputation. Society, manifesting itself politically, made him sheriff; society, manifesting itself ecclesiastically, made him deacon. Society seldom fails to smile on systematic courtship.

The old man continued to go his way here and there, giving account of himself to no one, contented enough no doubt to have one reputable son who looked after his own children and paid steady rent for, or bought piece by piece, the land he used; and another floating between the Rockies and the Mississippi, whose doings were of no importance in the village of Salem. But I doubt, on the whole, whether he was softened in heart by the deacon's manner or the ordering of the deacon's life to reflect unfilially on his own. Without claiming any great knowledge of the proprieties, he may have thought the conduct of his younger son the more filial of the two. Such was the history of the farmhouse between the years '56 and '82.

One wet April day, the sixth of the month, in the year '82, R. Rand went grimly elsewhere—where, his neighbors had little doubt. With true New England caution we will say that he went to the cemetery, the little grass-grown cemetery of Salem, with its meagre memorials and absurd, pathetic epitaphs. The minister preached a funeral sermon, out of deference to his deacon, in which he said nothing whatever about R. Rand, deceased; and R. Rand, sheriff and deacon, reigned in his stead.

Follow certain documents and one statement of fact:

Document 1.

Codicil to the Will of R. Rand.

The Will shall stand as above, to wit, my son, Robert Rand, sole legatee, failing the following condition: namely, I bequeath all my property as above mentioned, with the exception of this house and farm, to my son, Thomas Rand, provided, that within three months of the present date he returns and mends with his own hands the front window, third from the north, previously broken by him.

(Signed) R. Rand.

Statement of fact. On the morning of the day following the funeral the "condition" appeared in singularly problematical shape, the broken window, third from the north, having been in fact promptly replaced *by the hands of Deacon Rand himself.* The new pane stared defiantly across the lake, westward.

Document 2.

Leadville, Cal., May 15.

Dear Bob: I hear the old man is gone. Saw it in a paper. I reckon maybe I didn't treat him any squarer than he did me. I'll go halves on a bang-up good monument, anyhow. Can we settle affairs without my coming East? How are you, Bob?

Tom.

Document 3.

Salem, May 29.

Dear Brother: The conditions of our father's will are such, I am compelled to inform you, as to result in leaving the property wholly to me. My duty to a large and growing family gives me no choice but to accept it as it stands, and I trust and have no doubt that you will regard that result with fortitude. I remain yours,

Robert Rand.

Document 4.

Leadville, June 9.

A. L. Moore.

Dear Sir: I have your name as a lawyer in Wimberton. Think likely there isn't any other. If you did not draw up the will of R. Rand, Salem, can you forward this letter to the man who did? If you did, will you tell me what in thunder it was?

Yours, Thomas Rand.

Document 5.

Wimberton, June 18.

Thomas Rand.

Dear Sir: I did draw your father's will and enclose copy of the same, with its codicil, which may truly be called remarkable. I think it right to add, that the window in question has been mended by your brother, with evident purpose. Your letter comes opportunely, my efforts to find you having been heretofore unsuccessful. I will add further, that I think the case actionable, to say the least. In case you should see fit to contest, your immediate return is of course necessary. Very truly yours,

A. L. Moore,

Attorney-at-Law.

Document 6. Despatch.

New York, July 5.

To Robert Rand, Salem.

Will be at Valley Station to-morrow. Meet me or not.

T. Rand.

The deacon was a tall meagre man with a goatee that seemed to accentuate him, to hint by its mere straightness at sharp decision, an unwavering line of rectitude.

He drove westward in his buckboard that hot summer afternoon, the 6th of July. The yellow road was empty before him all the length of the lake, except for the butterflies bobbing around in the sunshine. His lips looked even more secretive than usual: a discouraging man to see, if one were to come to him in a companionable mood desiring comments.

Opposite the spring he drew up, hearing the sound of a hand-organ under the trees. The tall man with a clipped mustache sat up deliberately and looked at him. The leathery ape ceased his funereal capers and also looked at him; then retreated behind the spring. Pietro gazed back and forth between the deacon and the ape, dismissed his professional smile, and followed the ape. The tall man pulled his legs under him and got up.

"I reckon it's Bob," he said. "It's free quarters, Bob. Entrez. Come in. Have a drink."

The deacon's embarrassment, if he had any, only showed itself in an extra stiffening of the back.

"The train—I did not suppose—I was going to meet you."

"Just so. I came by way of Wimberton."

The younger brother stretched himself again beside the spring and drew his hat over his eyes. The elder stood up straight and not altogether unimpressive in front of it. Pietro in the rear of the spring reflected at this point that he and the ape could conduct a livelier conversation if it were left to them. Pietro could not imagine a conversation in which it was not desirable to be lively. The silence was long and, Pietro thought, not pleasant.

"Bob," said the apparent sleeper at last, "ever hear of the prodigal son?"

The deacon frowned sharply, but said nothing. The other lifted the edge of his hat brim.

"Never heard of him? Oh—have I Then I won't tell about him. Too long. That elder brother, now, he had good points;—no doubt of it, eh?"

"I confess I don't see your object—"

"Don't? Well, I was just saying he had good points. I suppose he and the prodigal had an average good time together, knockin' around, stubbin' their toes, fishin' maybe, gettin' licked at inconvenient times, hookin' apples most anytime. That sort of thing. Just so. He had something of an argument. Now, the prodigal had no end of fun, and the elder brother stayed at home and chopped wood; understood himself to be cultivating the old man. I take it he didn't have a very soft job of it?"—lifting his hat brim once more.

The deacon said nothing, but observed the hat brim.

"Now I think of it, maybe strenuous sobriety wasn't a thing he naturally liked any more than the prodigal did. I've a notion there was more family likeness between 'em than other folks thought. What might be your idea?"

The deacon still stood rigidly with his hands clasped behind him.

"I would rather," he said, "you would explain yourself without parable. You received my letter. It referred to our father's will. I have received a telegram which I take to be threatening."

The other sat up and pulled a large satchel around from behind him.

"You're a man of business, Bob," he said cheerfully. "I like you, Bob. That's so. That will—I've got it in my pocket. Now, Bob, I take it you've got some cards, else you're putting up a creditable bluff. I play this here Will, Codicil attached. You play,—window already mended; time expired at twelve o'clock to-night. Good cards, Bob—first-rate. I play here"—opening the satchel— "two panes of glass—allowin' for accidents—putty, et cetera, proposing to bust that window again. Good cards, Bob. How are you coming on?"

The deacon's sallow cheeks flushed and his eyes glittered. Something came into his face which suggested the family likeness. He drew a paper from his inner coat pocket, bent forward stiffly and laid it on the grass.

"Sheriff's warrant," he said, "for—hem—covering possible trespassing on my premises; good for twenty-four hours' detention—hem."

"Good," said his brother briskly. "I admire you, Bob. I'll be blessed if I don't. I play again." He drew a revolver and placed it on top of the glass. "Six-shooter. Good for two hours' stand-off."

"Hem," said the deacon. "Warrant will be enlarged to cover the carrying of concealed weapons. Being myself the sheriff of this town, it is—hem—permissible for me." He placed a revolver on top of the warrant.

"Bob," said his brother, in huge delight, "I'm proud of you. But—I judge you ain't on to the practical drop. *Stand back there!*" The deacon looked into the muzzle of the steady revolver covering him, and retreated a step, breathing hard. Tom Rand sprang to his feet, and the two faced each other, the deacon looking as dangerous a man as the Westerner.

Suddenly, the wheezy hand-organ beyond the spring began, seemingly trying to play two tunes at once, with Pietro turning the crank as desperately as if the muzzle of the revolver were pointed at him.

"Hi, you monk! Dance!" cried Pietro; and the leathery ape footed it solemnly. The perspiration poured down Pietro's face. Over the faces of the two stern men fronting each other a smile came and broadened slowly, first over the younger's, then over the deacon's.

The deacon's smile died out first. He sat down on a rock, hid his face and groaned.

"I'm an evil-minded man," he said; "I'm beaten."

The other cocked his head on one side and listened. "Know what that tune is, Bob? I don't."

He sat down in the old place again, took up the panes of glass and the copy of the will, hesitated, and put them down.

"I don't reckon you're beaten, Bob. You ain't got to the end of your hand yet. Got any children, Bob? Yes; said you had."

"Five."

"Call it a draw, Bob; I'll go you halves, counting in the monument."

But the deacon only muttered to himself: "I'm an evil-minded man."

Tom Rand meditatively wrapped the two documents around the revolvers.

"Here, Dago, you drop 'em in the spring!" which Pietro did, perspiring freely. "Shake all that. Come along."

The two walked slowly toward the yellow road. Pietro raised his voice despairingly. "No cent! Not a nicka!"

"That's so," said Tom, pausing. "Five, by thunder! Come along, Dago. It's free quarters. Entrez. Take a seat."

The breeze was blowing up over Elbow Lake, and the butterflies bobbed about in the sunshine, as they drove along the yellow road. Pietro sat at the back of the buck-board, the leathery ape on his knee and a smile on his face, broad, non-professional, and consisting largely of front teeth.

CONLON

CONLON, the strong, lay sick unto death with fever. The Water Commissioners sent champagne to express their sympathy. It was an unforced impulse of feeling.

But Conlon knew nothing of it. His lips were white, his cheeks sunken; his eyes glared and wandered; he muttered, and clutched with his big fingers at nothing visible.

The doctor worked all day to force a perspiration. At six o'clock he said: "I'm done. Send for the priest."

When Kelly and Simon Harding came, Father Ryan and the doctor were going down the steps.

"'Tis a solemn duty ye have, Kelly," said the priest, "to watch the last moments of a dying man, now made ready for his end."

"Ah, not Conlon! He'll not give up, not him," cried Kelly, "the shtrong man wid the will in him!"

"An' what's the sthrength of man in the hands of his Creathor?" said the priest, turning to Harding, oratorically.

"I don' know," said Harding, calmly. "Do you?"

"'Tis naught!"

Kelly murmured submissively.

"Kind of monarchical institution, ain't it, what Conlon's run up against?" Harding remarked. "Give him a fair show in a caucus, an' he'd win, sure."

"He'll die if he don't sweat," said the doctor, wiping his forehead. "It's hot enough." Conlon lay muttering and glaring at the ceiling. The big knuckles of his hands stood out like rope-knots. His wife nodded to Kelly and Harding, and went out. She was a good-looking woman, large, massive, muscular. Kelly looked after her, rubbing his short nose and blinking his watery eyes. He was small, with stooping shoulders, affectionate eyes, wavering knees. He had followed Conlon, the strong, and served him many years. Admiration of Conlon was a strenuous business in which to be engaged.

"Ah!" he said, "his wife ten year, an' me his inchimate friend."

It was ten by the clock. The subsiding noise of the city came up over housetops and vacant lots. The windows of the sickroom looked off the verge of a bluff; one saw the lights of the little city below, the lights of the stars above, and the hot black night between.

Kelly and Harding sat down by a window, facing each other. The lamplight was dim. A screen shaded it from the bed, where Conlon muttered and cried out faintly, intermittently, as though in conversation with some one who was present only to himself. His voice was like the ghost or shadow of a voice, not a whisper, but strained of all resonance. One might fancy him standing on the bank of the deadly river and talking across to some one beyond the fog, and fancy that the voices would so creep through the fog stealthily, not leaping distances like earthly sounds, but struggling slowly through nameless obstruction.

Kelly rubbed his hands before the fire.

"I was his inchimate friend."

Harding said: "Are you going to talk like a blanked idiot all night, or leave off maybe about twelve?"

"I know ye for a hard man, too, Simmy," said Kelly, pathetically; "an' 'tis the nathur of men, for an Irishman is betther for blow-in' off his shteam, be it the wrath or the sorrow of him, an' the Yankee is betther for bottlin' it up."

"Uses it for driving his engine mostly."

"So. But Conlon—"

"Conlon," said Harding slowly, "that's so. He had steam to drive with, and steam to blow with, and plenty left over to toot his whistle and scald his fingers and ache in his belly. Expanding that there figure, he carried suction after him like the 1:40 express, he did."

"'Tis thrue." Kelly leaned forward and lowered his voice. "I mind me when I first saw him I hadn't seen him before, unless so be when he was puttin' the wather-main through the sand-hills up the river an' bossin' a gang o' men with a fog-horn voice till they didn't own their souls, an' they didn't have any, what's more, the dirty Polocks. But he come into me shop one day, an' did I want the job o' plumbin' the court-house?

"'Have ye the court-house in your pocket?' says I, jokin'.

"'I have,' says he, onexpected, 'an' any plumbin' that's done for the court-house is done in the prisint risidence of the same.'

"An' I looks up, an' 'O me God!' I says to meself, "tis a man!' wid the black eyebrows of him, an' the shoulders an' the legs of him. An' he took me into the shwale of his wake from that day to this. But I niver thought to see him die."

"That's so. You been his heeler straight through. I don't know but I like your saying so. But I don't see the how. Why, look here; when I bid for the old water contract he comes and offers to sell it to me, sort of personal asset. I don't know how. By the unbroke faces of the other Water Commissioners he didn't use his pile-driving fist to persuade 'em, and what I paid him was no more'n comfortable for himself. How'd he fetch it? How'd he do those things? Why, look here, Kelly, ain't he bullied you? Ain't you done dirty jobs for him, and small thanks?"

"I have that."

Kelly's hands trembled. He was bowed down and thoughtful, but not angry. "Suppose I ask you what for?"

"Suppose ye do. Suppose I don' know. Maybe he was born to be king over me. Maybe he wasn't. But I know he was a mastherful man, an' he's dyin' here, an' me blood's sour an' me bones sad wid thinkin' of it. Don' throuble me, Simmy."

Harding leaned back in his chair and stared at the ceiling, where the lamp made a nebulous circle of light.

"Why, that's so," he said at last, in conclusion of some unmentioned train of thought. "Why, I got a pup at home, and his affection ain't measured by the bones he's had, nor the licks he's had, not either of 'em."

Kelly was deep in a reverie.

"Nor it ain't measured by my virtues. Look here, now; I don' see what his measure is."

"Hey?" Kelly roused himself.

"Oh, I was just thinking."

Harding thought he had known other men who had had in some degree a magnetic power that seemed to consist in mere stormy energy of initiative. They were like strong drink to weaker men. It was more physical than mental. Conlon was to Kelly a stimulant, then an appetite. And Conlon was a bad lot. Fellows that had heeled for him were mostly either wrecked or dead now. Why, there was a chap named Patterson that used to be decent till he struck Conlon, when he went pretty low; and Nora Reimer drowned herself on account of Patterson, when he got himself shot in a row at some shanty up the railroad. The last had seemed a good enough riddance. But Nora went off her head and jumped in the new reservoir. Harding remembered it the more from being one of the Water Company. They had had to empty the reservoir, which was expensive. And there were others. A black, blustering sort of beast, Conlon. He had more steam than was natural. Harding wondered vaguely at Kelly, who was spelling out the doctor's directions from a piece of paper.

"A powdher an' five dhrops from the short bottle. 'Tis no tin-course dinner wid the champagne an' entries he's givin' Conlon the night. Hey? A powdher an' five dhrops from the short bottle."

Harding's mind wandered on among memories of the little city below, an intricate, irregular history, full of incidents, stories that were never finished or dribbled off anywhere, black spots that he knew of in white lives, white spots in dark lives. He did not happen to know any white spots on Conlon.

"Course if a man ain't in politics for his health he ain't in it for the health of the community, either, and that's all right. And if he opens the morning by clumping Mrs. Conlon on the head, why, she clumps him back more or less, and that's all right." Then, if he went down-town and lied here and there ingeniously in the way of business, and came home at night pretty drunk, but no more than was popular with his constituency, why, Conlon's life was some cluttered, but never dull. Still, Harding's own ways being quieter and less cluttered, he felt that if Conlon were going off naturally now, it was not, on the whole, a bad idea. It would conduce to quietness. It would perhaps be a pity if anything interfered.

The clock in a distant steeple struck twelve, a dull, unechoing sound.

"Simmy," said Kelly, pointing with his thumb, "what do he be sayin', talkin'—talkin' like one end of a tiliphone?"

They both turned toward the bed and listened.

"Telephone! Likely there's a party at the other end, then. Where's the other end?"

"I don' know," whispered Kelly. "But I have this in me head, for ye know, when the priest has done his last, 'tis sure he's dhropped his man at the front door of wherever he's goin', wid a letther of inthroduction in his hatband. An' while the man was waitin' for the same to be read an' him certified a thrue corpse, if he had a kettleful of boilin' impatience in himself like Tom Conlon, wouldn't he be passin' the time o' day through the keyhole wid his friends be-yant?"

"'Tain't a telephone, then? It's a keyhole, hey?"

"Tiliphone or keyhole, he'd be talkin' through it, Conlon would, do ye mind?"

Harding looked with some interest. Conlon muttered, and stopped, and muttered again. Harding rose and walked to the bed. Kelly followed tremulously.

"Listen, will ye?" said Kelly, suddenly leaning down.

"I don' know," said Harding, with an instinct of hesitation. "I don' know as it's a square game. Maybe he's talkin' of things that ain't healthy to mention. Maybe he's plugged somebody some time, or broke a bank—ain't any more'n likely. What of it?"

"Listen, will ye?"

"Don' squat on a man when he's down, Kelly."

"'Sh!"

"*Hold Tom's hand. Wait for Tom,*" babbled the ghostly voice, a thin, distant sound.

"What'd he say? What'd he say?" Kelly was white and trembling.

Harding stood up and rubbed his chin reflectively. He did not seem to himself to make it out. He brought a chair, sat down, and leaned close to Conlon to study the matter.

"*What's the heart-scald, mother?*" babbled Conlon. "*Where'd ye get it from? Me! Wirra!*"

"'Tis spheakin' to ghosteses he is, Simmy, ye take me worrd."

"Come off! He's harking back when he was a kid."

Kelly shook his head solemnly.

"He's spheakin' to ghosteses."

"*What's that, mother? Arra! I'm sick, mother. What for? I don' see. Where'm I goin'?*"

"You got me," muttered Harding. "I don' know."

"*Tom'll be good. It's main dark. Hold Tom's hand.*"

Kelly was on his knees, saying prayers at terrific speed.

"Hear to him!" he stopped to whisper. "Ghosteses! Ora pro nobis—"

"*Tom ain't afraid. Naw, he ain't afraid.*"

Harding went back to his window. The air was heavy and motionless, the stars a little dim. He could see the dark line of the river with an occasional glint upon it, and the outline of the hills beyond.

The little city had drawn a robe of innocent obscurity over it. Only a malicious sparkle gleamed here and there. He thought he knew that city inside and out, from end to end. He had lived in it, dealt with it, loved it, cheated it, helped to build it, shared its fortunes. Who knew it better than he? But every now and then it surprised with some hidden detail or some impulse of civic emotion. And Kelly and Conlon, surely he knew them, as men may know men. But he never had thought to see Conlon as to-night. It was odd. But there was some fact in the social constitution, in human nature, at the basis of all the outward oddities of each.

"Maybe when a man's gettin' down to his reckonin' it's needful to show up what he's got at the bottom. Then he begins to peel off layers of himself like an onion, and 'less there ain't anything to him but layers, by and by he comes to something that resembles a sort of aboriginal boy, which is mostly askin' questions and bein' surprised."

Maybe there was more boyishness in Conlon than in most men. Come to think of it, there was. Conlon's leadership was ever of the maybe-you-think-I-can't-lick-you order; and men followed him, admitting that he could, in admiration and simplicity. You might see the same thing in the public-school yard. Maybe that was the reason. The sins of Conlon were not sophisticated.

The low, irregular murmur from the bed, the heavy heat of the night, made Harding drowsy. Kelly repeating the formula of his prayers, a kind of incantation against ghosts, Conlon with his gaunt face in the shadow and his big hands on the sheet clutching at nothing visible, both faded away, and Harding fell asleep.

He woke with a start. Kelly was dancing about the bed idiotically.

"He's shweatin'!" he gabbled. "He's shweatin'! He'll be well—Conlon."

It made Harding think of the "pup," and how he would dance about him, when he went home, in the crude expression of joy. Conlon's face was damp. He muttered no more. They piled the blankets on him till the perspiration stood out in drops. Conlon breathed softly and slept. Kelly babbled gently, "Conlon! Conlon!"

Harding went back to the window and rubbed his eyes sleepily.

"Kind of too bad, after all that trouble to get him peeled."

The morning was breaking, solemn, noiseless, with lifted banners and wide pageantries, over river and city.

Harding yawned.

"It's one on Father Ryan, anyway. That's a good thing. Blamed old windbag!"

Kelly murmured ecstatically, "Conlon will get well—Conlon!"

ST CATHERINE'S

ST. CATHERINE'S was the life work of an old priest, who is remembered now and presently will be forgotten. There are gargoyles over the entrance aside, with their mouths open to express astonishment. They spout rain water at times, but you need not get under them; and there are towers, and buttresses, a great clock, a gilded cross, and roofs that go dimly heavenward.

St. Catherine's is new. The neighborhood squats around it in different pathetic attitudes. Opposite is the saloon of the wooden-legged man; then the three groceries whose cabbages all look unpleasant; the parochial school with the green lattice; and all those little wooden houses—where lives, for instance, the dressmaker who funnily calls herself "Modiste." Beyond the street the land drops down to the freight yards.

But Father Connell died about the time they finished the east oriel, and Father Harra reigned over the house of the old man's dreams—a red-faced man, a high feeder, who looked as new as the church and said the virtues of Father Connell were reducing his flesh. That would seem to be no harm; but Father Harra meant it humorously. Father Connell had stumped about too much among the workmen in the cold and wet, else there had been no need of his dying at eighty-eight. His tall black hat became a relic that hung in the tiring room, and he cackled no more in his thin voice the noble Latin of the service. Peace to his soul! The last order he wrote related to the position of the Christ figure and the inscription, "Come unto me, weary and heavy-laden: I will give you rest." But the figure was not in place till the mid-December following.

And it was the day before Christmas that Father Harra had a fine service, with his boy choir and all; and Chubby Locke sang a solo, "Angels ever bright and fair," that was all dripping with tears, so to speak. Chubby Locke was an imp too. All around the altar the candles were lighted, and there hung a cluster of gas jets over the head of the Christ figure on the edge of the south transept. So fine it was that Father Harra came out of his room into the aisle (when the people were gone, saying how fine it was, and the sexton was putting out the gas here and there), to walk up and down and think about it, especially how he should keep up with the virtues of Father Connell. Duskier and duskier it grew, as the candles went out cluster by cluster till only those in the south transept were left; and Dennis, coming there, stopped and grunted.

"What!" said Father Harra.

"It's asleep he is," said the sexton. "It's a b'y, yer riverence."

"Why, so it is! He went to sleep during the service. H'm—well—they often do that, Dennis."

"Anyways he don't belong here," said Dennis.

"Think so? I don't know about that. Wait a bit. I don't know about that Dennis."

The boy lay curled up on the seat—a newsboy, by the papers that had slipped from his arms. But he did not look businesslike, and he did not suggest the advantages of being poor in America. One does not become a capitalist or president by going to church and to sleep in the best of business hours, from four to six, when the streets are stirring with men on their way to dinners, cigars and evening papers. The steps of St. Catherine's are not a bad place to sell papers after Vespers, and one might as well go in, to be sure, and be warm while the service lasts; only, as I said, if one falls asleep, one does not become a capitalist or president immediately. Father Harra considered, and Dennis waited respectfully.

"It's making plans I am against your natural rest, Dennis. I'm that inconsiderate of your feelings to think of keeping St. Catherine's open this night. And why? Look ye, Dennis. St. Catherine's is getting itself consecrated these days, being new, and of course—But I tell ye, Dennis, it's a straight church doctrine that the blessings of the poor are a good assistance to the holy wather."

"An' me wid children of me own to be missin' their father this Christmas Eve!" began Dennis indignantly.

"Who wouldn't mind, the little villains, if their father had another dollar of Christmas morning to buy 'em presents."

"Ah, well," said the sexton, "yer riverence is that persuadin'."

"It's plain enough for ye to see yourself, Dennis, though thick-headed somewhat. There you are: 'Come unto me, weary and heavy-laden;' and here he is. Plain enough. And who are the weary and heavy-laden in this city?"

"Yer riverence will be meanin' everybody," chuckled Dennis.

"Think so? Rich and poor and all? Stuff! I don't believe it. Not to-night. It'll be the outcasts, I'm thinking, Dennis. Come on."

"An' the b'y, yer riverence?"

"The what? Oh, why, yes, yes. He's all right. I don't see anything the matter with him. He's come."

It was better weather to go with the wind than against it, for the snow drove in gritty particles, and the sidewalks made themselves disagreeable and apt to slip out from under a person. Little spurts of snow danced up St. Catherine's roofs and went off the ridgepoles in puffs. It ought to snow on Christmas Eve; but it rightly should snow with better manners and not be so cold. The groceries closed early. Freiburger, the saloon man, looked over the curtains of his window.

"I don't know vat for Fater Harra tack up dings dis time by his kirch door, 'Come—come in here.' Himmel! der Irishman!"

Father Harra turned in to his supper, and thought how he would trouble Father Conner's reputation for enterprise and what a fine bit of constructive ability himself was possessed of.

The great central door of St. Catherine's stood open, so that the drift blew in and piled in windrows on the cold floor of the vestibule. The tall front of the church went up into the darkness, pointing to no visible stars; but over the doors two gas jets flickered across the big sign they use for fairs at the parochial school. "Come in here." The vestibule was dark, barring another gas jet over a side door, with another sign, "Come in here," and within the great church was dark as well, except for a cluster over the Christ figure. That was all; but Father Harra thought it a neat symbol, looking toward those who go from meagre light to light through the darkness.

Little noises were in the church all night far up in the pitch darkness of rafter and buttress, as if people were whispering and crying softly to one another. Now and again, too, the swing door would open and remain so for a moment, suspicious, hesitating. But what they did, or who they were that opened it, could hardly be told in the dusk and distance. Dennis went to sleep in a chair by the chancel rail, and did not care what they did or who they were, granted they kept away from the chancel.

How the wind blew!—and the snow tapped impatiently at stained windows with a multitude of little fingers. But if the noises among the rafters were not merely echoes of the crying and calling wind without, if any presences moved and whispered there, and looked down on flat floor and straight lines of pews, they must have seen the Christ figure, with welcoming hands, dominant by reason of the light about it; and, just on the edge of the circle of light, shapeless things stretched on cushions of pews, and motionless or stirring uneasily. Something now came dimly up the aisle from the swing door, stopped at a pew, and hesitated.

"Git out!" growled a hoarse voice. "Dis my bunk."

The intruder gave a nervous giggle. "Begawd!" muttered the hoarse voice. "It's a lady!"

Another voice said something angrily. "Well," said the first, "it ain't behavin' nice to come into me boodwer."

The owner of the giggle had slipped away and disappeared in a distant pew. In another pew to the right of the aisle a smaller shadow whispered to another:

"Jimmy, that's a statoo up there."

"Who?"

"That. I bet 'e's a king."

"Aw, no 'e ain't. Kings has crowns an' wallups folks."

"Gorry! What for?"

"I don' know."

The other sighed plaintively. "I thought 'e might be a king."

The rest were mainly silent. Some one had a bad cough. Once a sleeper rolled from the seat and fell heavily to the floor. There was an oath or two, a smothered laugh, and the distant owner of the giggle used it nervously. The last was an uncanny sound. The wakened sleeper objected to it. He said he would "like to get hold of her," and then lay down cautiously on his cushion.

Architects have found that their art is cunning to play tricks with them; whence come whispering galleries, comers of echoes, roofs that crush the voice of the speaker, and roofs that enlarge it. Father Connell gave no orders to shape the roofs of St. Catherine's, that on stormy nights so many odd noises might congregate there, whispering, calling, murmuring, now over the chancel, now the organ, now far up in the secret high places of the roof, now seeming to gather in confidence above the Christ figure and the circle of sleepers; or, if one vaguely imagined some inquisitively errant beings moving overhead, it would seem that newcomers constantly entered, to whom it had all to be explained.

But against that eager motion in the darkness above the Christ figure below was bright in his long garment, and quiet and secure. The cluster of gas jets over his head made light but a little distance around, then softened the dusk for another distance, and beyond seemed not to touch the darkness at all. The dusk was a debatable space. The sleepers all lay in the debatable space. They may have sought it by instinct; but the more one looked at them the more they seemed like dull, half-animate things, over whom the light and the darkness made their own compromises and the people up in the roof their own comments.

The clock in the steeple struck the hours; in the church the tremble was felt more than the sound was heard. The chimes each hour started their message, "Good will and peace;" but the wind went after it and howled it down, and the snow did not cease its petulance at the windows.

The clock in the steeple struck five. The man with the hoarse voice sat up, leaned over the back of the seat and touched his neighbor, who rose noiselessly, a huge fat man and unkempt.

"Time to slope," whispered the first, motioning toward the chancel.

The other followed his motion.

"What's up there?"

"You're ignorance, you are. That's where they gives the show. There's pickin's there."

The two slipped out and stole up the aisle with a peculiar noiseless tread. Even Fat Bill's step could not be heard a rod away. The aisle entered the circle of light before the Christ figure; but the two thieves glided through without haste and without looking up. The smaller, in front, drew up at the end of the aisle, and Fat Bill ran into him. Dennis sat in his chair against the chancel rail, asleep.

"Get onto his whiskers, Bill. Mebbe you'll have to stuff them whiskers down his throat."

There was a nervous giggle behind them. Fat Bill shot into a pew, dragging his comrade after him, and crouched down. "It ain't no use," he whispered, shaking the other angrily. "Church business is bad luck. I alius said so. What's for them blemed noises all night? How'd come they stick that thing up there with the gas over it? What for'd they leave the doors open, an' tell ye to come in, an' keep their damn devils gigglin' around? 'Taint straight I won't stand it."

"It's only a woman, Bill," said the other patiently.

He rose on his knees and looked over the back of the seat. "'Tain't straight. I won't stand it."

"We won't fight, Bill. We'll get out, if you say so."

The owner of the giggle was sitting up, as they glided back, Fat Bill leading.

- 75 -

"I'll smash yer face," the smaller man said to her.

Bill turned and grabbed his collar.

"You come along."

The woman stared stupidly after, till the swing door closed behind them. Then she put on her hat, decorated with too many disorderly flowers. Most of the sleepers were wakened. The wind outside had died in the night, and the church was quite still. A man in a dress suit and overcoat sat up in a pew beneath a window, and stared about him. His silk hat lay on the floor. He leaned over the back of the seat and spoke to his neighbor, a tramp in checked trousers.

"How'd I g-get here?" he asked thickly.

"Don' know, pardner," said the tramp cheerfully. "Floated in, same as me?" He caught sight of the white tie and shirt front. "Maybe you'd give a cove a shiner to steady ye out They don't give breakfasts with lodgin's here."

The woman with the giggle and the broken-down flowers on her hat went out next; then a tall, thin man with a beard and a cough; the newsboy with his papers shuffled after, his shoes being too large; then a lame man— something seemed the matter with his hip; and a decent-looking woman, who wore a faded shawl over her head and kept it drawn across her face—she seemed ashamed to be there, as if it did not appear to her a respectable place; last, two boys, one of them small, but rather stunted than very young. He said:

"'E ain't a king, is 'e, Jimmy? You don' know who 'e is, do you, Jimmy?"

"Naw."

"Say, Jimmy, it was warm, warn't it?"

Dennis came down the aisle, put out the gas, and began to brush the cushions. The clock struck a quarter of six, and Father Harra came in.

"Christmas, Dennis, Christmas! H'm—anybody been here? What did they think of it?"

Dennis rubbed his nose sheepishly.

"They wint to shleep, sor, an'—an' thin they wint out."

Father Harra looked up at the Christ figure and stroked his red chin.

"I fancied they might see the point," he said slowly. "Well, well, I hope they were warm."

The colored lights from the east oriel fell over the Christ figure and gave it a cheerful look; and from other windows blue and yellow and magical deep-sea tints floated in the air, as if those who had whispered unseen in the darkness were now wandering about, silent but curiously visible.

"Yer riverince," said Dennis, "will not be forgettin' me dollar."

THE SPIRAL STONE

THE graveyard on the brow of the hill was white with snow. The marbles were white, the evergreens black. One tall spiral stone stood painfully near the centre. The little brown church outside the gates turned its face in the more comfortable direction of the village.

Only three were out among the graves: "Ambrose Chillingworth, ætat 30, 1675;"

"Margaret Vane, ætat 19, 1839;" and "Thy Little One, O God, ætat 2," from the Mercer Lot. It is called the "Mercer Lot," but the Mercers are all dead or gone from the village.

The Little One trotted around busily, putting his tiny finger in the letterings and patting the faces of the cherubs. The other two sat on the base of the spiral, which twisted in the moonlight over them.

"I wonder why it is?" Margaret said. "Most of them never come out at all. We and the Little One come out so often. You were wise and learned. I knew so little. Will you tell me?"

"Learning is not wisdom," Ambrose answered. "But of this matter it was said that our containment in the grave depended on the spirit in which we departed. I made certain researches. It appeared by common report that only those came out whom desperate sin tormented, or labors incomplete and great desire at the point of death made restless. I had doubts the matter were more subtle, the reasons of it reaching out distantly." He sighed faintly, following with his eyes, tomb by tomb, the broad white path that dropped down the hillside to the church. "I desired greatly to live."

"I, too. Is it because we desired it so much, then? But the Little One"—

"I do not know," he said.

The Little One trotted gravely here and there, seeming to know very well what he was about, and presently came to the spiral stone. The lettering on it was new, and there was no cherub. He dropped down suddenly on the snow, with a faint whimper. His small feet came out from under his gown, as he sat upright, gazing at the letters with round troubled eyes, and up to the top of the monument for the solution of some unstated problem.

"The stone is but newly placed," said Ambrose, "and the newcomer would seem to be of those who rest in peace."

They went and sat down on either side of him, on the snow. The peculiar cutting of the stone, with spirally ascending lines, together with the moon's illusion, gave it a semblance of motion. Something twisted and climbed continually, and vanished continually from the point. But the base was broad, square, and heavily lettered: "John Mareschelli Vane."

"Vane? That was thy name," said Ambrose.

1890. Ætat 72.

An Eminent Citizen, a Public Benefactor, and Widely Esteemed.

For the Love of his Native Place returned to lay his Dust therein.

The Just Made Perfect.

"It would seem he did well, and rounded his labors to a goodly end, lying down among his kindred as a sheaf that is garnered in the autumn. He was fortunate."

And Margaret spoke, in the thin, emotionless voice which those who are long in the graveyard use: "He was my brother."

"Thy brother?" said Ambrose.

The Little One looked up and down the spiral with wide eyes. The other two looked past it into the deep white valley, where the river, covered with ice and snow, was marked only by the lines of skeleton willows and poplars. A night wind, listless but continual, stirred the evergreens. The moon swung low over the opposite hills, and for a moment slipped behind a cloud.

"Says it not so, 'For the Love of his Native Place'?" murmured Ambrose.

And as the moon came out, there leaned against the pedestal, pointing with a finger at the epitaph, one that seemed an old man, with bowed shoulders and keen, restless face, but in his manner cowed and weary.

"It is a lie," he said slowly. "I hated it, Margaret. I came because Ellen Mercer called me."

"Ellen isn't buried here."

"Not here!"

"Not here."

"Was it you, then, Margaret? Why?"

"I didn't call you."

"Who then?" he shrieked. "Who called me?"

The night wind moved on monotonously, and the moonlight was undisturbed, like glassy water.

"When I came away," she said, "I thought you would marry her. You didn't, then? But why should she call you?"

"I left the village suddenly!" he cried. "I grew to dread, and then to hate it. I buried myself from the knowledge of it, and the memory of it was my enemy. I wished for a distant death, and these fifty years have heard the summons to come and lay my bones in this graveyard. I thought it was Ellen. You, sir, wear an antique dress; you have been long in this strange existence. Can you tell who called me? If not Ellen, where is Ellen?" He wrung his hands, and rocked to and fro.

"The mystery is with the dead as with the living," said Ambrose. "The shadows of the future and the past come among us. We look in their eyes, and understand them not. Now and again there is a call even here, and the grave is henceforth untenanted of its spirit. Here, too, we know a necessity which binds us, which speaks not with audible voice and will not be questioned."

"But tell me," moaned the other, "does the weight of sin depend upon its consequences? Then what weight do I bear? I do not know whether it was ruin or death, or a thing gone by and forgotten. Is there no answer here to this?"

"Death is but a step in the process of life," answered Ambrose. "I know not if any are ruined or anything forgotten. Look up, to the order of the stars, an handwriting on the wall of the firmament. But who hath read it? Mark this night wind, a still small voice. But what speaketh it? The earth is clothed in white garments as a bride. What mean the ceremonials of the seasons? The will from without is only known as it is manifested. Nor does it manifest where the consequences of the deed end or its causes began. Have they any end or a beginning? I cannot answer you."

"Who called me, Margaret?"

And she said again monotonously, "I didn't call you."

The Little One sat between Ambrose and Margaret, chuckling to himself and gazing up at the newcomer, who suddenly bent forward and looked into his eyes, with a gasp.

"What is this?" he whispered. "'Thy Little One, O God, ætat 2,' from the Mercer Lot," returned Ambrose gently. "He is very quiet. Art not neglecting thy business, Little One? The lower walks are unvisited to-night."

"They are Ellen's eyes!" cried the other, moaning and rocking. "Did you call me? Were you mine?"

"It is, written, 'Thy Little One, O God,'" murmured Ambrose.

But the Little One only curled his feet up under his gown, and now chuckled contentedly.

THE MUSIDORA SONNET

THE clock in some invisible steeple struck one. The great snowflakes fell thickly, wavering and shrinking, delicate, barren seeds, conscious of their unfruitfulness. The sputter of the arc lights seemed explosive to the muffled silence of the street. With a bright corner at either end, the block was a canon, a passage in a nether world of lurking ghosts, where a frightened gaslight trembled, hesitated midway. And Noel Endicott conceived suddenly, between curb and curb, a sonnet, to be entitled "Dante in Tenth Street," the appearance of it occupying, in black letter, a half page in the *Monthly Illustrated*, a gloomy pencilling above, and below it "Noel Endicott." The noiselessness of his steps enlarged his imagination.

I walked in 19th Street, not the Florentine,

With ghosts more sad, and one like Beatrice

Laid on my lips the sanction of her kiss.

'Twas——

It should be in a purgatorial key, in effect something cold, white and spiritual, portraying "her" with Dantesque symbolism, a definite being, a vision with a name. "'Twas—" In fact, who was she?

He stopped. Tenth Street was worth more than a sonnet's confined austerity. It should be a story. Noel was one who beat tragic conceptions into manuscript, suffering rejection for improbability. Great actions thrilled him, great desires and despairs. The massive villainies of Borgia had fallen in days when art was strenuous. Of old, men threw a world away for a passion, an ambition. Intense and abundant life—one was compelled now to spin their symbols out of thin air, be rejected for improbability, and in the midst of a bold conception, in a snowstorm on canoned Tenth Street, be hungry and smitten with doubts of one's landlady.

Mrs. Tibbett had been sharp that morning relative to a bill, and he had remonstrated but too rashly: "Why discuss it, Mrs. Tibbett? It's a negative, an unfruitful subject." And she had, in effect, raved, and without doubt now had locked the outer door. Her temper, roused at one o'clock, would be hasty in action, final in result.

He stood still and looked about him. Counting two half blocks as one, it was now one block to Mrs. Tibbett and that ambushed tragedy.

In his last novel, "The Sunless Treasure" (to his own mind his greatest), young Humphrey stands but a moment hesitating before the oaken door, believing his enemies to be behind it with ready daggers. He hesitates but a moment. The die is cast. He enters. His enemies are not there. But Mrs. Tibbett seemed different. For instance, she would be there.

The house frontage of this, like the house frontage of the fatal next block, was various, of brick, brownstone or dingy white surface, with doorways at the top of high steps, doorways on the ground level, doorways flush with the front, or sunken in pits. Not a light in any window, not a battlement that on its restless front bore a star, but each house stood grim as Child Roland's squat tower. The incessant snowflakes fell past, no motion or method of any Byzantine palace intrigue so silken, so noiseless, so mysterious in beginnings and results. All these locked caskets wedged together contained problems and solutions, to which Bassanio's was a simple chance of three with a pointed hint. Noel decided that Tenth Street was too large for a story. It was a literature. One must select.

Meanwhile the snow fell and lay thickly, and there was no doubt that by persistent standing in the snow one's feet became wet. He stepped into the nearest doorway, which was on the level of the street, one of three doorways alike, all low, arched and deep.

They would be less noticeable in the daytime than in the night, when their cavernous gaping and exact repetition seemed either ominous or grotesque, according to the observer. The outer door was open. He felt his way in beyond the drift to the hard footing of the vestibule, kicked his shoes free of snow and brushed his beard.

The heroes of novels were sometimes hungry and houseless, but it seemed to Noel that they seldom or never faced a problem such as Mrs. Tibbett presented. Desperate fortunes should be carried on the point of one's sword, but with Mrs. Tibbett the point was not to provoke her. She was incongruous. She must be thrust aside, put out of the plot. He made a gesture dismissing Mrs. Tibbett. His hand in the darkness struck the jamb of the inner door, which swung back with a click of the half-caught latch. His heart thumped, and he peered into the darkness, where a thin yellow pencil of light stretched level from a keyhole at the farther end of a long hall.

Dismissing Mrs. Tibbett, it was a position of dramatic advantage to stand in so dark and deep an arched entrance, between the silence and incessant motion of the snow on the one hand, and the yellow pencil of light, pointing significantly to something unknown, some crisis of fortune. He felt himself in a tale that had both force and form, responsible for its progress.

He stepped in, closed the half door behind him softly, and crept through the hall. The thin line of light barred the way, and seemed to say, "Here is the place. Be bold, ready-minded, full of subtlety and resource." There was no sound within that he could hear, and no sound without, except his own oppressed breathing and pulses throbbing in his ears.

Faint heart never won anything, and as for luck, it belonged to those who adventured with various chances, and of the blind paths that led away from their feet into the future, chose one, and another, and so kept on good terms with possibility. If one but cried saucily, "Open this odd little box, you three gray women!" And this, and this the gray Fates smiled indulgently, showing a latent motherliness. How many destinies had been decided by the opening and shutting of a door, which to better or worse, never opened again for retreat? A touch on this door and Mrs. Tibbett might vanish from the story forever, to the benefit of the story.

He lifted his hand, having in mind to tap lightly, with tact and insinuation, but struck the door, in fact, nervously, with a bang that echoed in the hall. Some one spoke within. He opened and made entry in a prepared manner, which gave way to merely blinking wonder.

It was a large dining-room, brightly lit by a chandelier, warm from a glowing grate, sumptuous with pictures and hangings, on the table a glitter of glass and silver, with meat, cakes and wine.

On the farther side of the table stood a woman in a black evening dress, with jewels on her hair and bosom. She seemed to have just risen, and grasped the back of her chair with one hand, while the other held open a book on the table. The length of her white arm was in relief against her black dress.

Noel's artistic slouch hat, now taken off with uncertain hand, showed wavy brown hair over eyes not at all threatening, a beard pointed, somewhat profuse, a face interestingly featured and astonished. No mental preparation to meet whatever came, of Arabic or mediaeval incident, availed him. He felt dumb, futile, blinking. The lady's surprise, the startled fear on her face, was hardly seen before it changed to relief, as if the apparition of Noel, compared with some foreboding of her own, were a mild event. She half smiled when he began:—

"I am an intruder, madam," and stopped with that embarrassed platitude. "I passed your first door by accident, and your second by impulse."

"That doesn't explain why you stay."

"May I stay to explain?"

When two have exchanged remarks that touch the borders of wit, they have passed a mental introduction. To each the mind of the other is a possible shade and bubbling spring by the dusty road of conversation. Noel felt the occasion. He bowed with a side sweep of his hat.

"Madam, I am a writer of poems, essays, stories. If you ask, What do I write in poems, essays, stories, I answer, My perception of things. If you ask, In what form would I cast my present perceptions of things, I say, Without doubt a poem."

"You are able to carry both sides of a conversation. I have not asked any of these."

"You have asked why I stay. I am explaining."

The lady's attitude relaxed its stiffness by a shade, her half smile became a degree more balmy.

"I think you must be a successful writer."

"You touch the point," he said slowly. "I am not. I am hungry and probably houseless. And worse than that, I find hunger and houselessness are sordid, tame. The taste of them in the mouth is flat, like stale beer. It is not like the bitter tang of a new experience, but like something the world shows its weariness of in me."

The amused smile vanished in large-eyed surprise, and something more than surprise, as if his words gave her some intimate, personal information.

"You say strange things in a very strange way. And you came in by an accident?"

"And an impulse?"

"I don't understand. But you must sit down, and I can find you more to eat, if this isn't enough."

Noel could not have explained the strangeness of his language, if it was strange, further than that he felt the need of saying something in order to find an opportunity of saying something to the point, and so digplayed whatever came to his mind as likely to arrest attention. It was a critical lesson in vagabondage, as familiar there as hunger and houselessness. He attacked the cold meat, cakes and fruit with fervor, and the claret in the decanter. But what should be the next step in the pursuit of fortune? At this point should there not come some revelation?

The lady did not seem to think so, but sat looking now at Noel and now at her own white hands in her lap. That she should have youth and beauty seemed to Noel as native to the issue as her jewels, the heavy curtains, the silver and glass. As for youth, she might be twenty, twenty-one, two. All such ages, he observed to himself with a mental flourish, were one in beauty. It was not a rosy loveliness like the claret in the decanter, nor plump like the fruit in the silver basket, but dark-eyed, white and slender, with black hair drawn across the temples; of a fragile delicacy like the snowflakes, the frost flower of the century's culture, the symbol of its ultimate luxury. The rich room was her setting. She was the center and reason for it, and the yellow point of a diamond over her heart, glittering, but with a certain mellowness, was still more central, intimate, interpretative, symbolic of all desirable things. He began to see the story in it, to glow with the idea.

"Madam," he said, "I am a writer of whose importance I have not as yet been able to persuade the public. The way I should naturally have gone to-night seemed to me something to avoid. I took another, which brought me here. The charm of existence—" She seemed curiously attentive. "The charm of existence is the unforeseen, and of all things our moods are the most unforeseen. One's plans are not always and altogether futile. If you propose to have salad for lunch, and see your way to it, it is not so improbable that you will have salad for lunch. But if you prefigure how it will all seem to you at lunch, you are never quite right. Man proposes and God disposes. I add that there is a third and final disposal, namely, what man is to think of the disposition after it is made. I hope, since you proposed or prefigured to-night, perhaps as I did, something different from this—this disposition"—he lifted his glass of claret between him and the light—"that your disposition what to think of it is, perhaps, something like mine."

The lady was leaning forward with parted lips, listening intently, absorbed in his words. For the life of him Noel could not see why she should be absorbed in his words, but the fact filled him with happy pride.

"Tell me," she said quickly. "You speak so well—"

Noel filled in her pause of hesitation.

"That means that my wisdom may be all in my mouth."

"No, indeed! I mean you must have experience. Will you tell me, is it so dreadful not to have money? People say different things."

"They do." He felt elevated, borne along on a wave of ornamental expression. "It is their salvation. Their common proverbs contradict each other. A man looks after his pence and trusts one proverb that the pounds will look after themselves, till presently he is called penny wise and pound foolish, and brought up by another. And consider how less noticeable life would be without its jostle of opinion, its conflicting lines of wisdom, its following of one truth to meet with another going a different way. Give me for finest companionship some half truth, some ironic veracity."

She shook her head. It came to him with a shock that it was not his ornamental expression which interested her, but only as it might bear on something in her own mind more simple, direct and serious, something not yet disclosed. "In fact," he thought, "she is right. One must get on with the plot" It was a grievous literary fault to break continuity, to be led away from the issue by niceties of expression. The proper issue of a plot was simple, direct, serious, drawn from the motive which began it. Why did she sit here with her jewels, her white arms and black dress these weird, still hours of the night? Propriety hinted his withdrawal, but one must resist the commonplace.

"The answer to the question does not satisfy you. But do you not see that I only enlarged on your own answer? People say different things because they are different. The answer depends on temperaments, more narrowly on moods; on tenses, too, whether it is present poverty and houselessness or past or future. And so it has to be answered particularly, and you haven't made me able to answer it particularly to you. And then one wouldn't imagine it could be a question particular to you."

"You are very clever," she murmured, half smiling again. "Are you not too clever for the purpose? You say so many things."

"That is true," said Noel plaintively. "The story has come to a standstill. It has all run out into diction."

At that moment there was a loud noise in the hall.

The smile, which began hopefully, grew old while he watched it, and withered away. The noise that echoed in the hall was of a banging door, then of laden, dragging steps. The hall door was thrown open, and two snowy hackmen entered, holding up between them a man wearing a tall hat.

"He's some loaded, ma'am," said one of them cheerfully. "I ain't seen him so chucked in six months."

They dropped him in a chair, from which, after looking about him with half-open, glassy eyes, and closing them again, he slid limply to the floor. The hackman regarded that choice of position with sympathy.

"Wants to rest his load, he does," and backed out of the door with his companion.

"It goes on the bill. Ain't seen him so chucked in six months."

The lady had not moved from her chair, but had sat white and still, looking down into her lap. She gave a hard little laugh.

"Isn't it nice he's so 'chucked'? He would have acted dreadfully." She was leaning on the table now, her dark eyes reading him intently. The man on the floor snorted and gurgled in his sleep.

"I couldn't kill anybody," she said. "Could you?"

Noel shook his head.

"It's so funny," she went on in a soft, speculative way, "one can't do it. I'm afraid to go away and be alone and poor. I wish he would die."

"It wouldn't work out that way," said Noel, struggling with his wits. "He's too healthy."

It seemed to him immediately that the comment was not the right one. It was not even an impersonal fact to himself, an advantage merely to the plot, that the sleeper was unable to object to him and discard him from it, as he had resolved to discard Mrs. Tibbett, but with such brutal energy as the sleeper's face indicated. For it repelled not so much by its present relaxed degradation as by its power, its solidity of flesh, its intolerant self-assertion, the physical vigor of the short bull neck, bulky shoulders, heavy mustache, heavy cheeks and jaw, bluish with the shaving of a thick growth. He was dressed, barring his damp dishevelment, like a well-groomed clubman.

But the lady was looking Noel in the eyes, and her own seemed strangely large, but as if covering a spiritual rather than a physical space, settled in melancholy, full of clouds, moving lights and dusky distances.

"I was waiting for him because he ordered me. I'm so afraid of him," she said, shrinking with the words. "He likes me to be here and afraid of him."

"Tell me what I am to do?" he said eagerly.

"I suppose you are not to do anything."

Noel caught the thread of his fluency. He drew a ten-cent piece from his pocket, tossed it on the table, gestured toward it with one hand and swung the other over the back of his chair with an air of polished recklessness.

"But your case seems desperate to you. Is it more than mine? You have followed this thing about to 'the end of the passage,' and there is my last coin. My luck might change to-morrow. Who knows? Perhaps tonight. I would take it without question and full of hope. Will you experiment with fortune and—and me?"

The dark eyes neither consented nor refused. They looked at him gravely.

"It is a black, cold night. The snow is thick in the air and deep on the street Put it so at the worst, but fortune and wit will go far."

"Your wit goes farther than your fortune, doesn't it?" she said, smiling.

"I don't conceal."

"You don't conceal either of them, do you? You spread them both out," and she laughed a pleasant little ripple of sound.

Noel rose with distinction and bent toward her across the table.

"My fortune is this ten-cent piece. As you see, on the front of it is stamped a throned woman."

"Oh, how clever." She laughed, and Noel flushed with the applause.

"Shall we trust fortune and spin the coin? Heads, the throned woman, I shall presently worship you, an earthly divinity. Tails, a barren wreath and the denomination of a money value, meaning I take my fortunes away, and you," pointing in turn to the sleeper and the jewels, "put up with yours as you can."

She seemed to shiver as he pointed. "No," she said, "I couldn't do that. A woman never likes to spin a coin seriously."

"Will you go, then?"

The sleeper grunted and turned over. She turned pale, put her hand to her throat, said hurriedly, "Wait here," and left the room, lifting and drawing her skirt aside as she passed the sleeper.

She opened the door at last and came again, wrapped in a fur mantle, carrying a travelling case, and stood looking down at the sleeper as if with some struggle of the soul, some reluctant surrender.

They went out, shutting the door behind them.

The snow was falling still on Tenth Street, out of the crowding night. He held her hand on his arm close to him. She glided beside him noiselessly.

The express office was at the corner, a little dingy, gas-lit room.

"Carriage? Get it in a minute," said the sleepy clerk. "It's just round the corner."

They stood together by a window, half opaque with dust. Her face was turned away, and he watched the slant of her white cheek.

"You will have so much to tell me," he whispered at last.

"I am really very grateful. You helped me to resolve."

"Your carriage, sir."

The electric light sputtered over them standing on the curb.

"But," she said, smiling up at him, "I have nothing to tell you. There is nothing more. It ends here. Forgive me. It is my plot and it wouldn't work out your way. There are too many conflicting lines of wisdom in your way.

My life lately has been what you would call, perhaps, a study in realism, and you want me to be, perhaps, a symbolic romance. I am sure you would express it very cleverly. But I think one lives by taking resolutions rather than by spinning coins, which promise either a throned woman, or a wreath and the denomination of a money value. One turns up so much that is none of these things. Men don't treat women that way. I married to be rich, and was very wretched, and perhaps your fame, when it comes, will be as sad to you. Perhaps the trouble lies in what you called 'the third disposal.' But I did not like being a study in realism. I should not mind being something symbolic, if I might prove my gratitude"—she took her hand from his arm, put one foot on the step and laughed, a pleasant little ripple of sound—"by becoming literary material." The door shut to, and the carriage moved away into the storm with a muffled roll of wheels.

Noel stared after it blankly, and then looked around him. It was half a block now to Mrs. Tibbett. He walked on mechanically, and mounted the steps by habit. The outer door was not locked. A touch of compunction had visited Mrs. Tibbett.

He crept into his bed, and lay noting the growing warmth and sense of sleep, and wondering whether that arched doorway was the third of the three or the second. Strictly speaking he seemed to have gone in at the middle one and come out at the third, or was it not the first rather than the middle entrance that he had sheltered in? The three arched entrances capered and contorted before him in the dark, piled themselves into the portal of a Moorish palace, twisted themselves in a kind of mystical trinity and seal of Solomon, floated apart and became thin, filmy, crescent moons over a frozen sea. He sat up in bed and smote the coverlet.

"I don't know her name! She never told me!" He clutched his hair, and then released it cautiously. "It's Musidora! I forgot that sonnet!"

'Twas Musidora, whom the mystic nine

Gave to my soul to be forever mine,

And, as through shadows manifold of Dis,

Showed in her eyes, through dusky distances

And clouds, the moving lights about their shrine;

Now ever on my soul her touch shall be

As on the cheek are touches of the snow,

Incessant, cool, and gone; so guiding me

From sorrow's house and triple portico.

And prone recumbrance of brute tyranny,

In a strict path shall teach my feet to go.

The clock in the invisible steeple struck three.

———————————————

Milton Keynes UK
Ingram Content Group UK Ltd.
UKHW011124180424
441376UK00004B/197